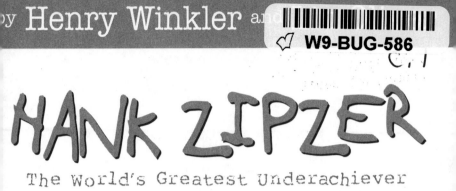

by Henry Winkler and

W9-BUG-586

HANK ZIPZER

The World's Greatest Underachiever

Dump Trucks and Dogsleds:

I'm on My Way, Mom!

Grosset & Dunlap

Cover illustration by Jesse Joshua Watson

GROSSET & DUNLAP
Published by the Penguin Group
Penguin Group (USA) Inc., 375 Hudson Street, New York, New York 10014, USA
Penguin Group (Canada), 90 Eglinton Avenue East, Suite 700, Toronto,
Ontario M4P 2Y3, Canada
(a division of Pearson Penguin Canada Inc.)
Penguin Books Ltd., 80 Strand, London WC2R 0RL, England
Penguin Group Ireland, 25 St. Stephen's Green, Dublin 2, Ireland
(a division of Penguin Books Ltd.)
Penguin Group (Australia), 250 Camberwell Road, Camberwell, Victoria 3124, Australia
(a division of Pearson Australia Group Pty. Ltd.)
Penguin Books India Pvt. Ltd., 11 Community Centre, Panchsheel Park,
New Delhi—110 017, India
Penguin Group (NZ), 67 Apollo Drive, Rosedale, North Shore 0745,
Auckland, New Zealand
(a division of Pearson New Zealand Ltd.)
Penguin Books (South Africa) (Pty.) Ltd., 24 Sturdee Avenue,
Rosebank, Johannesburg 2196, South Africa

Penguin Books Ltd., Registered Offices: 80 Strand, London WC2R 0RL, England

Text copyright © 2009 by Henry Winkler and Lin Oliver Productions, Inc. Illustrations
copyright © 2009 by Penguin Group (USA) Inc. All rights reserved. Published by Grosset
& Dunlap, a division of Penguin Young Readers Group, 345 Hudson Street, New York,
New York 10014. GROSSET & DUNLAP is a trademark of Penguin Group (USA) Inc.
Printed in the U.S.A.

Library of Congress Control Number: 2009010173

ISBN 978-0-448-44380-5 (pbk)   10 9 8 7 6 5 4 3 2 1
ISBN 978-0-448-44381-2 (hc)   10 9 8 7 6 5 4 3 2 1

For Stacey with love.—H.W.

*For Jan Platt . . . my generous, brave
and darling friend.—L.O.*

CHAPTER 1

"I'm not moving! And neither are my underpants, so put them right back in the drawer where they belong, Mom. Please!"

My parents were in my room, moving all my stuff around like I wasn't even there. They had already emptied out the drawer with my Mets sweatshirt collection and were cramming perfectly good Mets gear into the drawer with my boxer shorts, which were already squeezed in next to my pajamas. Can you believe that?

"Hank," my mom answered without even looking up. "We're not asking you to move. We're just asking you to move *over*."

"The baby is due very soon, Hank," my dad chimed in. "And he has to sleep somewhere. It's perfectly obvious that we only have a three bedroom apartment."

"Fine," I said. "Then let the little ankle-biter sleep in Emily's room. Or better yet, why don't we move Emily out, all the way to Aunt Maxine's on Long Island? Then the baby will have his own room, and he'll be the happiest little guy in New York. Or if that doesn't work, I'm sure Katherine will be happy to make room for him in her glass cage."

"It makes much more sense for you two brothers to share a room and let Emily have her own room," my dad said.

"Maybe that makes sense to you, Dad, but not to me."

"Hank, honey. I can hear you're upset." My mom tousled my hair like she always does, but this time it didn't help at all. "You're going to be the big brother. Just think, the new baby is going to look up to you and admire you and learn so many things from you."

My mom had been saying that line for the past six months, and I stopped believing it four and a half months ago. I don't know if you've ever gotten a new baby in your house, but if you have, then you know parents will say almost anything to convince you that its arrival is going to be the greatest thing since the invention of video games. But we big brothers and sisters know better, don't we?

I immediately went to my desk and opened the bottom drawer on the left. I think it was the left. If it wasn't the left, then it was definitely the right. It had to be one of the two. Anyway, I reached in, moved my baseball glove aside, lifted my New York Rangers signed hockey puck off my collection of slightly dented ping-pong balls, and finally found what I was looking for. It was the pink, rubberized nose clip I used when I was learning to do backflips in my diving class at the pool at the Y. I put it on my nose, and turned around to face my parents.

"What is the purpose of that?" my dad asked in a very irritated voice, which unfortunately for me, is not an unusual voice for him.

"Let's be honest, folks," I answered, sounding like I had the worst stuffy nose in the entire history of colds and the flu. "The main thing this baby is going to do in my room is stink it up. I've been around diapers a time or two, and they don't exactly smell like perfume."

"Stop being ridiculous and take that nose

3

clip off," my dad said. Stanley Zipzer is not big on humor, nose clip related or otherwise. "We have a lot to accomplish here, Hank."

"Please try to understand how I'm feeling, Dad," I reasoned. "Having a new baby was not exactly my idea. No one asked my opinion."

"Hank, honey," my mom began, but I wasn't done yet. I opened my mouth and more words came pouring out.

"Listen, Mom. It's not fair. I'm the one who has to move all my stuff and cut my room in half. And for what? I've never even met this kid. How do I know I'm going to like him?"

"Everybody loves their brothers and sisters," my mom said.

"Oh, really? Have they met Emily, lizard girl from Mars?"

"I don't like your attitude, Hank." My dad was getting really annoyed. "This is getting downright silly. The baby is moving in with you, and that's final."

"Stanley," my mom said to him. "Could Hank and I have a minute together? Just the two of us?"

"Sure," my dad answered. "I can get back

to my crossword puzzle. I only need three more downs and two acrosses."

Checking to see that he had his mechanical pencil tucked snuggly behind his ear, he made a beeline for his swivel recliner chair in the living room, where he spends many happy hours filling in such exciting clues as a seven-letter synonym for toenail clippings.

My mom patted the bed. "Come sit next to me, honey. I think we need to have a talk."

Uh-oh. Here it comes, Hank. She's going to talk about feelings, and you know what that means. Tears. Or at least wet eyes . . . hers. Happens every time.

"Are you feeling worried about the new baby?" she asked, sounding like she was going to cry already, and we hadn't even started talking.

"What I'm feeling worried about, Mom, is that I'm going to wind up living in the basement . . . or at least, visiting most of my stuff there."

"Adding a new member to our family will bring us all closer together, honey, even if it means making a few small sacrifices."

"So my small sacrifices are losing half my room, and never seeing you and Dad again because you're going to be busy feeding and burping and changing and pinching and cooing and . . ."

"I see where this is going, Hank," she said, taking my hand in hers. "You're concerned that you won't have as much time with us, that we'll be distracted by the baby. I understand your fears. And I have a promise and a suggestion. Which do you want to start with?"

"Let's go with the promise. It sounds promising."

Despite the serious tone going on in the room, I took a moment to crack myself up. I do enjoy the old Zipzer attitude, even under pressure.

"Well," my mom said when I had finished laughing. "I promise you that even after the baby comes, I will . . . let me rephrase that . . . we will be there for you no matter what, for whatever you need."

I have to admit, that did feel pretty good. I wasn't positive she could keep that promise, but my mom was starting to get wet from her tears, so I thought I better move right along to the suggestion. I just nodded my head like I was agreeing.

"Now for the suggestion part," my mom said. "How about if Dad takes you on a special trip for a few days?"

"Like now?"

"Like this weekend."

"Wow, Mom. That sounds cool. Wait a minute. Will my room be here when I get back?"

"Of course. If you guys go away, it will give me time to get ready for the baby. But more important, it will give you, your Dad, and your sister some special time together before the baby comes."

Wait another minute. Did she slip in the sister word? When did Emily get a ticket for this trip?

"Why do we have to take her?" I complained. "Emily doesn't need as much special time as I do."

"And why is that, honey?"

"Because she's happy spending time with just herself and her lizard pal. I'd be surprised if she even notices the new baby, unless he has 188 sharp teeth and scales."

"The baby is going to change everybody's lives, Hank," my mom said with a smile. "Even Emily's. But one thing is for sure, we'll all be the better for it."

I wasn't so sure of that. But I decided not to argue with her about it. I mean, she was really, really pregnant and everything.

Besides, I was getting a cool weekend trip out of it. Worse things could happen.

CHAPTER 2

Five minutes after my mom left my room, my dad came in and handed me a piece of lined, yellow notebook paper.

"Your mom told me about the trip," he said, "so I made you a list."

I snatched the paper from his hand, thinking he had made a list of all the cool destinations we could choose for our trip. This was going to be fun to read.

What was I thinking? Stanley Zipzer does not make fun lists.

What it turned out to be was a list of warm clothing, like my long underwear and my parka. I guess he could see I was kind of disappointed.

"It's a packing list," my dad said. "You know. Of things you should pack."

"Dad, not that this isn't a great list or

anything, and I really like your penmanship, but where am I wearing this stuff?"

"No questions allowed," my dad said. "It's a surprise."

"Just tell me, Dad. Is it a cool place?"

"Extremely, Hank."

Wow. My mind immediately went into overdrive. What kind of trip could my father have in mind? Remember, he didn't think it was just a regular cool place but an *extremely* cool place. To find out, we'd have to venture inside Stanley Zipzer's head. Come with me now and I'll take you there. I know it sounds scary, but don't worry. I'm going to stay with you for the entire tour.

TEN PLACES STANELY ZIPZER'S BRAIN THINKS WOULD MAKE A COOL TRIP

1. A visit inside the world's largest mechanical pencil to see how it works. (*Wow, that would be really dangerous. I mean, we could be rubbed out by the world's largest eraser.*)
2. A field trip to visit the "Dad's School of Boring Lectures About Why Homework

Should be Done Neatly and for At Least Twenty-Seven Hours a Day." (*Holy macaroni, rash bumps are sprouting all over my upper arm just thinking about it.*)

3. A spa just for dads where the only thing they do all day is fall asleep in a recliner in front of the television while scratching their butts and snoring. (*Count me out on that one. All I have to do is hike into the living room and I'm on that trip.*)

4. A crossword puzzle convention where you do nothing but work on crossword puzzles and eat pretzels that are shaped like all twenty-six letters of the alphabet. (*With my reading problems, I wouldn't be able to tell the difference between the B pretzels and the D pretzels because I get them so confused.*)

I don't know about you, but I'm not having a whole lot of fun here inside Stanley Zipzer's brain, so please follow me to the nearest exit and don't touch any of the furniture. (*Phew! I'm glad to be out of there. I'm used to my brain, which is pretty disorganized and scattered, but at least I have fun in there!*)

CHAPTER 3

I took my dad's list and walked into Emily's room. She was on the floor playing with her iguana, Katherine. And by playing, I mean she was teaching that scaly lizard to peel an orange.

"I hate to interrupt your girly snack time," I said.

"This is not snack time, Hank." Even though she was sitting down, Emily's voice sounded like she was standing over me with her hands on her hips, tapping her foot impatiently. That's the voice she saves just for me.

"If you had any sense," she went on, "you'd realize that this is emergency training. In case a volcano erupts and I'm stuck at school, I want Katherine to be able to create her own balanced meals."

I was about to tell her that the last time a

volcano erupted in New York was never, but then I came to my senses and thought: *No, Hank, don't even begin this conversation because it's going to lead you into Emilyville, which is an even scarier place to hang out than Stanley Zipzer's brain.*

So I got right down to business and waved Dad's list under Emily's nose.

"Did you get one of these?" I asked her.

"Of course I did. I'm going on the trip, too, you know. And so is Cheerio."

"Cheerio is going? You're kidding me."

"Hank, I don't kid."

As if I didn't know that. If there's one thing my sister Emily isn't, it's funny.

"Well, I'm glad Cheerio's coming," I said to her. "It's you I'm not so glad about."

"This trip is for us Zipzer kids," Emily said. "It's not just special Hank time."

"Ease up on the attitude, Em. All I was doing was coming in here to ask if you got the list."

"Yes, Hank, I did. And I'm already packed."

"Of course you are. You were born packed."

"Packing is simply a matter of organizing your thoughts, Hank. I think it's time you learned to do that."

My sister Emily is the total opposite of me. I try to be organized and she *is*. I try to spell and she *can*. I try to remember where I put my backpack and she *does*. I think you get the picture. I'm learning challenged and she's *not*, which is something she likes to bring up at least fifteen times a day.

I try to be like Emily, all organized and efficient and stuff. But I just can't pull it off. I wish I could be like her. I want to be like her. Dr. Berger, the school psychologist, has explained to me that my brain is just wired differently. I've come to accept that fact. I mean, I have no choice . . . unless I could go in there with a special brain screwdriver and re-wire it. Ouch, I don't like that thought.

"So, I suppose you're here to ask me to help you pack?" Emily asked.

"No," I snapped back. "I came in here to ask if you know where we're going."

"I don't, except that Dad said it was someplace extremely cool. So I'm hoping maybe it's to the regional meeting of the Association for the Protection of Iguanas and Bearded

14

Dragons."

Remember those left arm bumps from Stanley Zipzer's brain? They're back, but this time they're behind my knees. Call me crazy, but that's just the way Bearded Dragon conventions affect me.

As for me, I left the room.

But the truth is, I still needed help packing. Maybe for some of you, putting a bunch of stuff in a suitcase is easy, especially if you have a list. But for me, getting more than four items in and still being able to zip up the suitcase is downright hard. And one of those four items is not even my toothbrush.

Once our whole family went on a road trip down south for my dad to compete against the best crossword puzzlers in America. For the entire trip, I had to brush my teeth with my finger because I couldn't fit my toothbrush into my suitcase. Actually, brushing your teeth with your finger is kind of fun because you get to hear that clean squeak when your finger rubs against your front teeth. (My dentist, Dr. Crumbworthy is not a fan of the technique. He loves the combo of bristles and floss.)

Anyway, I still had the packing problem to deal with. To solve it, I called Frankie Townsend, my best friend, and Ashley Wong, my other best friend. I ask you . . . if your best friends can't help you pack, who can?

They were in the apartment almost before I hung up the phone. I'm really lucky to have two good friends who are always there to help me out. We went directly into my room.

I dragged down my sports equipment bag from the top shelf of my closet. It was full of stuff left over from who knows when. As I dumped it all on the floor, the baseball that I used when Papa Pete taught me how to pitch rolled out of the bag. Wow, that sucker had been missing for over a year.

Ashley got me organized right away. She is an excellent organizer. She assigned each of us a job. Frankie was to read the list. I was to get the items out that needed to be packed. And Ashley would put them into the suitcase.

"Parka," Frankie read, crossing off the first word on my dad's list.

I got my blue parka out of the closet and handed it to Ashley.

"You've got to be kidding," she said. "If I put this big, puffy jacket in the bag, there will be no room for anything, not even your tooth-brush."

"Now you tell me," I said. "Where were you when I went to the crossword puzzle contest?"

We decided I'd wear the parka instead of packing it.

"Snow boots, snow gloves, and knitted beanie," Frankie read from the list. "Where are you going, man? To the Arctic Circle? You better leave today. I hear the ice is melting fast up there."

"That's why my family recycles everything," Ashley said.

While Frankie and Ashley discussed what they were doing to prevent climate change, I dragged out my warmest snow clothes from the cedar chest in my closet. Ashley studied them for a minute, then picked up the boots. She put one boot on either side of the very bottom of the bag, which propped it open to make room for other things.

"Hank, watch how I'm doing this," she said.

I watched, amazed, as Ashley filled up one boot with my warm socks and the other boot with my pajamas that she rolled up tightly. It's funny how you can know someone all your life and not know what hidden talents they have.

With the help of Frankie and Ashley, I finally got my bag packed. I'm happy to report that I even got my toothbrush safely inside.

"Wow," Ashley said when we were finished. "I love going on trips. I wish my mom was having a baby so my dad would take me on a mystery trip."

"Trust me, Ashweena," I said to her. "You don't wish your mom was having a baby because before you know it, you'd be squished into *half* of your room and sitting on *half* of your desk chair because The Baby gets *half* of everything."

"Maybe having a little brother won't be so bad, Zip," Frankie said. "I'm a little brother, and look how cool I turned out to be."

"Ask your older brother Otis if he shares your opinion," I shot back.

"Now that you mention it, I think you might

be right," Frankie said. "Last week, he put blue masking tape right down the middle of our room and told me that his side of the room was a separate country and I didn't have a passport to enter."

My dad pushed open the door and came in. And let me just warn you, it wasn't a pretty sight. He was wearing a bright red and white, wooly snow cap with long tassels hanging down by his ears along with two huge, red pom-poms . . . and I'm talking blimp-sized, red pom-poms. He looked like a nerdy Santa Claus except with no presents and no reindeer.

"Tell me you're not wearing that on our trip, Dad," I said. "And tell me fast."

"What's wrong with this hat?" My dad caught a glimpse of himself in the mirror over my dresser, and flashed a crazy smile. "I found it buried under my college fencing equipment."

"And that's exactly where it needs to return," I told him.

"Wow, Mr. Z . . . you fenced in college?" Frankie asked.

"I'll have you know, I received a third place medal in men's sabre fencing."

With that, he lunged at Frankie, waving a pretend sword around like a madman. That move, combined with his bouncing red pom-pom hat and fluttering ear flaps, created a picture that I won't soon forget. I hope you never have that picture of your dad in your head.

"Frankie and Ashley really want to hear all about your fencing days, Dad. But maybe you can save the story for later. They were just leaving. Weren't you, guys?"

"Yes, Mr. Zipzer," Ashley said. "I have rhinestones waiting to be glued on a new pair of sneakers, and rhinestones don't like to be kept waiting, especially the purple ones."

"And I have . . . uh . . . some . . . uh . . . important stuff to do, too," Frankie added. "So important I can't even say how important it is."

Wow, Frankie was really struggling. I made a mental note to give him a few lessons in the old Hank Zipzer make-up-an-excuse-on-the-spot technique.

"It can wait until next time, kids," my dad told Frankie and Ashley. "I'll dig out my fencing gear and put on a real exhibition for you."

With that, he disappeared from the room with his red pom-poms following after him. We all breathed a sigh of relief.

"It's going to be a long three days," I said, shaking my head. "Between that hat, my dad's stories, and my sister Emily's attitude, maybe I should pack myself in a bag and ride in the trunk."

Frankie patted me on the back. "Hey, Zip. Relax and enjoy the trip. It's going to be your last couple days as the only boy in the Zipzer family."

Wow, that fact hit me like a ton of bricks.

I just sat there and let it all sink in. This baby, this brother, this crying little poop machine, really was going to arrive very soon now, whether I liked it or not.

CHAPTER 4

There's only one thing more boring than taking a long car trip with your dad and your sister and your dog, and that's telling someone else about it. So I'm going to do us both a huge favor, and just say this: We got there.

And there was . . . Vermont. Not just Vermont, but our family's favorite ski slopes just outside of a town called Randolph.

I hope you appreciate what I've done for you. Even though my car trip took six and a half hours, I got you there in two short paragraphs. So you owe me one. Big time.

CHAPTER 5

We checked in to the Don't Fall on Your Butt Motel.

Okay, it wasn't actually called that, but it should have been because that's the first thing I did when I stepped out of the car. Hey, no one told me that the entire state of Vermont is still covered with ice in the spring. Of course, someone must have told Emily, unless she just has a built-in ice detector, because the minute I landed on my butt, she said, "Everyone knows, Hank, you have to walk flat-footed and carefully on ice or you'll fall on your rump."

"Thank you, oh rump mistress," I said.

Then a great thing happened. The rump mistress herself went sliding on a puddle of black ice and landed smack on her . . . let's all say it together . . . RUMP!

I didn't just laugh; I snorted and howled like

a ticklish hyena.

"I don't see anything funny about this," Emily snarled.

"Trust me, Emily. This is not just funny, this is the king of comedy."

She tried to lunge for me, but all that did was send her right back where she belonged, sprawled out like a rag doll on the ice. Cheerio stuck his nose out of the car and looked at Emily laying there on the ground. He gave a little yip and started wagging his tail very fast. I believe that was his way of laughing at how ridiculous she looked. Seeing him so amused made Emily even madder.

Her face turned all red. She looked like she was about to start her fake crying routine. Fortunately, my dad reached out and pulled her up before the waterworks started. Like mother, like daughter.

"We're here to have fun, kids," he said. "Let's all try to get along. Now, both of you help me unload the luggage from the car."

Of course, I (being the boy) had to carry old Emily's bag up the stairs to our room. It weighed a ton.

"Don't let my duffel touch the ground," Emily commanded as I lugged it up the stairs. "I don't want it to get wet."

"What did you pack in there?" I grunted. "Boulders?"

"Use your head, Hank. Where would I get boulders in New York City? And besides, what would be the point of transporting large rocks to Vermont, where many types of geological boulders exist naturally in the landscape."

Some sense of humor that girl has, huh? I was going to point out to old Em that I didn't actually think she had packed large, brown rocks in her bag, but to be truthful, I didn't have the lungs to talk and carry her stupid bag upstairs at the same time.

We were in Room 23. The first thing I noticed as I walked inside was that Room 23 only had two beds. And did I mention . . . there were three of us? I'm no math genius; I think you know that by now. But even I could figure out that we were one bed short. When I pointed this out to my dad, he phoned downstairs to the motel desk and asked them to send up a rollaway cot.

They did, but it was not a great rollaway cot. In fact, it looked like it could roll away on its own at any minute. Emily and I flipped to see who was going to sleep on it, and wouldn't you know it, I lost.

My dad insisted we go to bed early, so we could wake up at the crack of dawn and hit the ski slopes before the crowds arrived. He and Emily went to sleep right away. Cheerio curled up on the pillow next to my dad and started to snore. But me, I couldn't find a comfortable position no matter what I did. I tossed all around that stupid rollaway cot, trying to find a place where there wasn't a spring poking some part of my body. I must have tossed one time too many because in the middle of the night, I awoke to find myself the bologna in a bed sandwich. By that I mean, the rollaway cot had snapped shut like a clamshell and trapped me in the middle.

"Help," I whimpered. "My bed is eating me."

No one answered. My dad just kept right on snoring, and Emily tossed the pillow over her head without even waking up. This called for the Hank Zipzer Big Voice.

"Help!" I shouted. "I'm trapped! Here!

Somebody! Hello!"

That did it. My dad woke up with a startle, flipped on the light, and squinted at me. Actually, he squinted at my forehead and my feet because the rest of me was caught in the middle of the bed.

"Stop clowning around, Hank," he said.

Why is it that even in an emergency, people think I'm clowning around? Like the time I tried to explain to my teacher Ms. Adolf that Cheerio really did eat the model I built of a Hopi kiva and got the toothpick ladder stuck in his throat and we had to go to the vet for emergency ladder removal. She didn't take me seriously at all and told me my sense of humor was wearing her nerves thin. I couldn't convince her that I wasn't kidding around, and it really did happen.

"I'm not clowning around, Dad," I said. "Could you just open the bed and get me out, and we'll discuss my sense of humor at a later time."

As my dad got out of bed and came over to rescue me, I noticed that he was wearing his red and white pom-pom hat. He must have slipped it on during the night, which I don't blame him for because it was as cold as an icebox in our room. But let me just say this: That hat definitely did not go with his boxer shorts. Or with anything else for that matter.

He pulled the two sides of the bed down and held it open just long enough for me to pop out. Wow, it felt good to be out of that mattress sandwich.

"Hank, if this bed isn't working out, you can sleep with me," he offered.

Okay. So there were my choices. Sleep in a bed that wants to eat me, or sleep with a billy goat, because I've done this once before, and my dad kicks like he has hooves instead of toes. And, I should add, he would be no ordinary billy goat but a billy goat in a ski hat.

I picked the boy-eating bed. My dad kicking like a goat I could have dealt with, but the red pom-pom hat was a deal breaker.

In the morning, a very not-rested me, an unusually quiet Emily, and an extremely silly-looking Dad made it to the ski lift before the crowds arrived. In fact, before *anyone* arrived. My dad likes to be prompt, which to him means getting places about a hundred hours before anyone else does. We left Cheerio back at the motel, fast asleep on my dad's pillow. He was the only one in the family who had the good sense to stay in bed on such a frosty morning.

While my Dad was buying the lift tickets, Emily and I waited to get fitted for our boots and skis. She didn't look happy, not that she ever does, but she looked especially sour that morning.

"What's the problem?" I asked her. "Missing your lizard?"

"I'm a little worried about Katherine," Emily said. "Separating from me gives her major anxiety attacks."

"How can you tell? Do her scales break out in a sweat?"

Emily didn't seem to hear what I said. She just kept staring out the window of the ski rental hut and looking up at the slopes. The first few skiers were lining up for the chair lift.

"That looks like total fun, doesn't it?" I commented.

She didn't answer. I noticed that her lips seemed tight, and formed a straight line like a ruler across her face.

"I thought you loved skiing," I said to her.

"I did last year when we went," Emily said. "This year, the mountain looks . . . I don't know . . . bigger. Taller. Steeper."

"News flash, Em. Mountains don't grow in a year. You're a big-time scientist, you should know that."

She just nodded. I have to confess, I felt a little sorry for her. I mean, here we were, off on a last fun fling before Mr. Poopy Pants arrived, and Emily was looking scared, like she had just seen the swamp creature from the green lagoon.

"Over here, kids," the guys at the ski hut called. "Let's get you measured for boots and skis."

"Give me really fast skis," I said to my guy, who was an older teenager with bright red hair the color of a ripe tomato. "I'm going to rip up that mountain."

"I'll take the slow ones," Emily said to her guy, who was an older man with a gray beard and leathery skin. Her voice sounded kind of shaky. "It's been a while since I skied."

"Take your time and get used to the snow," the man with the beard told us. "There's a big storm coming and it can get icy out there."

"I love ice," I said. "It makes you slide really fast."

"Actually, if a storm is coming, maybe we should just forget skiing," Emily said. "We could stay in and have hot chocolate."

"Don't worry. The storm's not supposed to get here before late afternoon," the leathery man said. "Still plenty of time for good skiing."

Emily didn't answer. She just swallowed hard, fidgeted with her ski gloves, and complained about her boots being too tight.

Once we got our boots on, we carried our poles and skis over to the ski lift line and met up with our dad. He didn't need to rent equipment, because he had brought his from home. I have to tell you, he put together one truly super-weird ski outfit. You already know about the red pom-pom hat. But he had added a pair of zebra-striped ski pants, a red ski jacket that was so shiny it actually glittered in the sunlight, and a pair of yellow ski goggles that made him look like a mutant grasshopper.

"Hey, kids. I have the lift tickets right here. Let's go. Let's go. If you listen very carefully, you can hear the mountain calling our names."

My dad was over-the-moon enthusiastic, like the way he gets when he finishes the Sunday crossword puzzle in under four minutes and thirty-eight seconds. I can't say the same for Emily. She looked pale and frightened. Wow, good old Emily had transformed from Miss Know-It-All to Miss I'm-So-Scared-I'm-Going-to-Cry-Any-Minute.

We stepped into our skis and waddled over to the chair lift.

"I'll jump on the first chair," my dad said. "You kids ride up together right behind me. We'll meet at the top."

"Do we have to go all the way to the top?" Emily asked.

"Sure," my dad said. "We're only on an intermediate slope. It's not that high. See you up there."

The chairlift swung around, and the attendant helped my dad onto the seat. As he pulled the safety bar across his zebra-striped pants, he turned around and hollered, "Is this a six-letter word for fun, or what?"

It was time for Emily and me to get on the lift. I walked out to the spot where you board, and when I turned to check for Emily, I noticed she wasn't next to me.

"Hurry up," I yelled over to her, "or we'll miss the chair."

Before she could answer, the attendant had taken her by the hand and pulled her out to where you catch the chair. As she plopped down on the bench, he pulled the safety bar down across us, and told us to hang on tight.

He didn't have to say that to Emily because she was already hanging on so tight, her knuckles were white. You could see that right through her puffy ski gloves.

"You okay?" I asked her as the chairlift made its way up the mountain.

"To tell you the truth, Hank, I'm feeling kind of scared. I don't like looking down. And I don't like looking up. And I especially don't like looking around."

"Then look at me," I said. "See how calm I am. There's nothing to worry about. You know how to do this."

"I wish . . ." she began. "I wish . . . I don't know what I wish."

I had never seen this side of her before, the side that doesn't know something. She seemed almost human.

"I know what we'll do," I said. "Let's sing. You can't be scared when you're singing. It's a proven fact."

With that, I burst into a really walloping version of "I've Been Working on the Railroad," blasting it out at the top of my lungs.

I've been working on the railroad
All the livelong day

The echo was so strong, it sounded like there was a whole bunch of us singing. To my astonishment, Emily joined in. We were singing our way up the mountain, when a *really* astonishing thing happened.

And hold on to your hats, folks, because you're not going to believe this. Emily Grace Zipzer actually reached out and took my hand.

Yup, that's what I said. Don't tell anyone, but I held her hand all the way to the top.

CHAPTER 6

By the time we reached the top of the mountain, I thought Emily had calmed down enough to be able to get off the chairlift. When you get to the top, all you have to do is lift up your bar and put your skis out in front of you. When your feet touch the snow, you stand up and glide down a small mound, which gets you out of the way of the next people getting off the lift.

I lifted the safety bar. So far, so good. I told Emily I would say "go" when it was time for her to stand up and ski down the little mound. I waited until just the right moment, and then as calmly as I could, I said, "Okay, Emily. Go."

She gave a little whimper, kind of like Cheerio does when he really wants a lamb chop but knows he's not supposed to beg. Then she slid off the chair seat and stood up on her skis. Again, so far, so good. She made it over the mound, getting out of the way of the next people.

But here's the problem—she couldn't stop.

I just stood there watching as she skied down the mound and slammed face first into the picket fence that surrounds the hot chocolate stand at the top of the mountain. As she crashed into the fence, her skis wedged perfectly between the slats. She actually looked like she had been built into the fence as a holiday decoration.

Her whimper turned into a scream.

"Hank!" she shrieked. "I'm stuck! Get me out of here!"

The sound of her scream was so high, I was afraid it might start an avalanche. I saw that once on the Discovery Channel on a show called *Man Against the Elements*.

Before I could get to her, my father was already there. He grabbed her by the back of her ski parka and yanked really hard. As she came loose from the picket fence, I could have sworn I heard a pop, like someone had opened a can of soda.

"There you go," my dad said. "Good as new."

"That's it, Dad," Emily cried. "I'm done skiing. I'll be right here having a hot chocolate with marshmallows. You guys come get me when you're done."

"Emily, you have to ski down," he informed her. "There's no other way."

"Yeah," I chimed in. "It's not like you can call a taxi and say drop me off at the bottom."

She gave me a dirty look.

"Hey, I'm just trying to be helpful. The truth is the truth. Look around. Do you see any other form of transportation?"

"I can't do it." Emily shook her head and planted her skis firmly in the snow. "My feet are frozen, and I don't mean cold. They won't move."

"This isn't like you, Emily," my dad said. "You're always so capable."

"Well, at this moment I'm incapable of moving."

"I have an idea," I said. It was a good thing, too, otherwise I could imagine us still standing there for the Fourth of July fireworks. "Dad will go first and ski very slowly in a downward direction."

I saw her eye twitch.

"But not too downward," I added quickly. "Then you'll follow him, staying very close so nothing bad can happen."

Yup, there went the other one. Now both her eyes were twitching.

"And I'll be right behind you, bringing up the rear. That way you'll be protected, like a baby iguana surrounded by grown-up iguanas."

I thought the iguana thing was a nice touch, to make her feel comfortable in her beloved reptile world.

"Don't even go there, Hank. Iguanas don't ski, and you know it."

Okay, the reptile thing didn't work, but you have to give me credit for trying.

"Come on, Emily. Be reasonable," my dad said. "Hank has a good idea. We'll get to the bottom safely, you can relax while Hank and I do a few more runs, and this afternoon, we'll do whatever you want."

Emily wasn't happy about the plan, but she finally had to agree to it. So we pointed our skis downward and turned the tips facing each other in what they call a snowplow, which is like skiing with brakes on, and began to make our way down the mountain. Emily actually was doing fine, and she was starting to relax. I could tell by the way her neck got longer as she un-hunched her shoulders and stopped looking like a tortoise.

Until . . . *Briiiiiiiiiiiiiiing. Briiiiiiiiiiiiiiiiiing.*

What was that?

Briiiiiiiiiiiiiiiiiiiiiiiiiiiiiing.

It was a cell phone ringing. Who carries a cell phone while they're skiing? I'll tell you who. My dad, that's who. I could see him fumbling in his parka pocket, trying to answer the phone.

"We have to stop for a minute, kids," he called out.

"I can't stop," Emily said. "Remember how I crashed into the fence."

"Well, I can't answer the phone while I'm skiing," my dad shouted back.

"You don't have to, Dad!" I called out. "The person will call back."

"What if it's your mother?" he shouted. "I promised her I'd be easy to reach."

He slowed down so much while he was talking, that Emily . . . sure enough . . . crashed into him. She got him smack in the back of the knees, and her skis tangled up with his until they both fell over into the bank of snow. Their legs were up in the air and their skis looked like four chopsticks stuck in a bowl of white rice.

I tried to avoid them, but I was so close that I tumbled right on top of them. Now there were six chopsticks sticking out of that bowl.

Briiiingggg. Briiiiiiing.

The phone was still ringing.

My dad stuck the fingers of his glove in his mouth, to try to pull it off so he could reach the phone. Emily was back to her whimpering, and I was rapidly getting in a bad mood because a pile of snow had wedged itself down my ski pants. I don't want to go into specifics here, but just think frozen underpants, and you're getting the picture.

My dad finally managed to dig the phone out of his pocket. He flipped it open, but before he got it to his ear, it slipped out of his hand and buried itself in the soft snow. It was still ringing. We could hear it but we couldn't see it.

I dug around in the snow, following the sound, and rescued it.

"Answer quickly," my dad said. "Before it stops ringing."

"Hello," I said. "Oh, hi Mom. How you doing? You are? It is? You're what? Now?"

Wow. This was too much information for me. I handed the phone to my dad.

"Hello, Randi? You are? It is? You're what? Now?"

Emily was going crazy.

"Will somebody please tell me what now means?" she said.

"It means Mom's on her way to the hospital," I said.

"Now?" she said.

"Now," I said.

CHAPTER 7

When Emily heard that my mom was on the way to the hospital, she rolled up into a ball right there on the snow. She looked like a doodlebug in a huge purple parka. I didn't know what was going on with her, but she definitely had gone into some kind of bizarro state of mind. It could have been fear, because your mom having a baby is a scary thing. It could have been shock, because it was very surprising that the baby was coming early. Or it could have been just Emily being weird Emily. She is certainly capable of being odd. Let's face it, folks. The girl talks to lizards.

Anyway, there she was, rolled up in the snow like a puffy, purple pea pod. I glanced over at my dad, and he looked confused. This is not a look you often see on Stanley Zipzer's face. My dad always knows exactly what should happen next. Like after dinner, you watch Jeopardy. Or after you eat your cereal, you rinse your dish and spoon and put them in the dishwasher. Or after you turn out the light at night, you put your head on the pillow and go to sleep. He's a guy who always knows what comes next.

But there he was, standing on that mountain in Vermont with Emily curled up at his feet and my mom on the way to the hospital, and he truly looked like he didn't know what to do next. I felt I needed to take charge.

"No one panic," I said. "There is no need for panic."

"I'm calm as a cucumber," my dad answered.

Yeah right. So why is he sitting there in the snow like Frosty the Snowman?

"Me too," a little voice said from deep inside the hood of the purple parka.

"Emily, if you're so calm, how come you're down there doing an impersonation of a dead doodlebug?"

She stuck her face out of her parka hood. "I believe you're referring to the pill bug," she said, "which, as everyone knows, is a member

43

of the woodlice family."

"This is no time for science, Emily," I said. "This is a time for standing up and getting down the mountain. Now give it a try."

"I'm comfortable here," she shot back.

My dad was still frozen in his same position. He didn't even seem to notice that his yellow ski goggles were all steamed up. Oh man. This was going to require some serious leadership on my part.

"Okay, everybody listen to me," I said, making my voice sound cool and collected, like I was the captain of an airplane. "Focus on my voice. Mom is having a baby, and she needs us to be there. And we're up here and we need to be down there. So we're just going to get down to the motel, pick up Cheerio and our things, and drive back to the City. No problem."

This seemed to snap my dad out of his trance.

"Good thinking, Hank," he said. "That's just what we'll do."

If I wasn't already sitting down, I would have fallen flat over. This was the first time ever that my dad had given me a compliment on my thinking. Usually, he just points out what a lousy thinker I am and says things like, "Use your head, Hank!" What do you think I was using, my elbow?

"Okay, Dad, you lead the way down the mountain," I announced. "Emily, you'll ski right in back of him, and I'll go last. When I count to three, everyone stand up. One. Two. Three."

Amazingly, on the count of three, my dad stood up and shook the snow off his zebra ski pants. Not amazingly, Emily remained seated.

"Emily, you have to do this," I reasoned. "Mom is counting on you."

"It's such a long way down, Hank."

"We'll go slowly."

"That's what you said last time, and I fell on my butt."

She did have a point there. But we had to get down, and we had to hurry. That guy at the ski rental place had said there was a storm coming in the afternoon, and we needed to be on the road to New York before it blew in. My mind raced. Finally, it raced right into a good idea.

"I have it, Emily. You'll butt ski down."

"I don't know how to butt ski. Besides,

Hank, there is no such thing. You're just making it up."

"Would I make up something like that? Everybody butt skis. It's the new snowboarding."

"Really, Hank?"

"Sure. You just crouch down and rest your backside on your skis. Then somebody else pulls you down the mountain. You can't fall down, because you're already down."

"Are you sure I won't look stupid?" Emily asked.

"Em, I ask you. Could a girl of your intelligence and grace and style ever look stupid?"

Between you and me, the answer is totally YES, YES, and YES.

But I didn't tell that to Emily because I needed her cooperation. So with great reluctance and even a few little tears brimming up in her beady eyes, Emily sat up, held on to my parka sleeve, and butt skied down the mountain.

CHAPTER 8

TEN DISADVANTAGES OF BUTT SKIING DOWN A MOUNTAIN

1. You look totally stupid.
2. Your skis keep falling off because they were meant to hold feet, not butt cheeks.
3. Everyone shouts this at you: *Hey, Knucklehead! You're supposed to stand up on those skis!*
4. It's wet. No way you can keep your rear end dry when you're dragging it along in the snow.
5. You leave butt tracks so even if people don't see you, they know you've been there. Enough said about that!
6. It takes a really long time. The human butt was definitely not built for speed.
7. The ski patrol stops you and asks if you're

okay, and you have to pretend that butt skiing is something you do every day.

8. Everyone snaps a picture of you and says, "I can't wait to post this on the Internet."

9. I wouldn't know this personally, but according to Emily, your butt nearly starts to freeze up like a bag of frozen peas and becomes numb.

10. Did I mention that you look totally stupid? Yeah, well that deserves to be said twice.

CHAPTER 9

Hats off to Emily, though. She toughed it out and got to the bottom of the mountain even though her butt skiing style created quite a ruckus among the skiers. We didn't care that everyone was staring at us, though. We just wanted to get out of there as fast as we could and get on the road to New York. There was a baby coming, and we weren't going to let my mom do this alone.

By the time we got back to the motel, my dad seemed to be functioning a little better. He called my mom on her cell phone to get more details. Frankie's mom was taking her to the hospital in a cab, and they were almost there. Emily and I gathered around my dad and tried to hear what she was saying, but he told us to get our things packed and he'd tell us everything when he hung up.

We raced around the room, gathering up our pajamas and toothbrushes and stray socks. Cheerio could tell something was up. He picks up on your mood really fast. If I'm nervous, he's nervous. If I'm tired, he's tired. If I'm hungry, he's hungry. Well actually, he's always hungry, so I guess that one doesn't count. As we raced around getting ready to leave, he started spinning in circles, chasing his tail at warp speed. He was going so fast, you couldn't tell his head from his tail.

"He's excited to be having a baby brother," Emily said.

"That's because he doesn't know about the stinky diaper part yet," I said.

"Hank, you are so gross."

"Hey, I'm not the gross one. It's not me who's going to the bathroom in my pants."

When my dad hung up the phone, he seemed a little more like himself. At least he was able to string a couple of sentences together. He told us that my mom's water had broken which meant she was going to have the baby pretty soon.

"What's plumbing got to do with having babies?" I asked. I remember one time, our neighbor Mrs. Fink's hot water pipe behind her sink had broken and I didn't notice her having any babies, just a flood.

"The baby floats in water inside Mom's tummy," Emily informed me. "When the bag of water breaks, it means the baby is ready to be born."

"How am I supposed to know that?" I asked.

"Because Mom has explained it to you a thousand times. If you ever listened, Hank, you'd know that."

Okay, I'll score that one point for Emily. Concentrating when people are explaining things to me is not one of my strong points.

Even though I hadn't really known the whole water deal before, I thought it was cool that my little brother was floating in water. That meant he had to be a good swimmer. Maybe he'd grow up to be in the Olympics one day. That would be exciting. I'd go see him and sit in the stands and cheer.

Oh wow. I sure hope he doesn't wear those skimpy, skintight Speedos that make it look like you have almost nothing on. That would be really embarrassing especially if they had an American flag on them. Hey, if he's in water now, will he come out with those on?

"HANK!" I heard my dad saying. "Let's go!"

From the tone of his voice, I could tell this wasn't the first time he'd called my name. I guess my brain had flown to the Olympics and, as usual, had forgotten to come back.

I grabbed my duffel and we hurried down the stairs to our car. The snow was starting to fall as we loaded our stuff into the minivan.

Correction. The snow wasn't falling. It was plunging down in thick blankets of huge, fat snowflakes. My dad went to pay the motel bill, and in just the few minutes that we waited for him, enough snow fell on the ground for Emily and me to make snow angels. And not just one angel. We made a whole flock of snow angels. Or maybe you call it a herd. Or a school. Or a pod. Anyway, I don't know what you call a big group of snow angels but I made a mental note to look it up when I got home.

My dad returned and we climbed into the backseat. We drove slowly out of the parking lot, hearing the snow and ice crunch under our tires. As we pulled out onto the highway, the snow was coming down so quickly, the windshield wipers couldn't clear if off the windows, even when they were going at the fastest speed. My dad was forced to drive really slowly.

We crept our way through town. A lot of snow was piling up in the middle of the road.

"I hope they plow these roads," my dad said. "It's getting pretty deep here."

I am not a person to be easily alarmed. In general, I am cool and unruffled, except in the case of spelling bees, pop math quizzes, and any other school type of test you can name. But I am here to tell you guys, as we left town and headed toward the highway, I felt my heart starting to pound. This was one alarming snowstorm. Driving down the highway, the snow was so thick you couldn't see five feet in front of you. We had no choice but to keep going even though I'm sure that cars were not built to travel sideways.

Within an hour, everything had turned white. The trees were white. The road was white. The houses were white. And my dad's face was white—with fear!

"You okay, Dad?" I asked from the back-seat.

"This is tough driving," he responded. "Not much visibility."

We had to stop a lot to clean off the front windshield.

"Maybe we should pull off the road and wait for the storm to pass over," Emily suggested.

"Right, and by that time, Mom will have had the baby and we'll be under a mountain of snow," I said. "Use your head, Emily."

We crept along the highway for another hour, but to be honest, we weren't making much progress. We were going slower than if we were walking. A couple of times my dad tried to speed up, but that made the back of the car fish-tail like one of those cars in the Indy 500. The road was slippery and snowy and we were the only car out there.

We got very quiet. The only thing you could hear was Cheerio snoring. He was curled up on my lap, unaware that my dad was driving along a road that he couldn't see. Sometimes, it's good to be a dog.

At last, we saw a town up ahead. It wasn't

much of a town, but there were lights on in some of the houses, and a little downtown street. We all breathed a sigh of relief as we approached the town. It was called Bedroom Falls or Bear Claw Falls or Belly Ache Falls . . . or something that started with a B. Sorry, but you know I'm not such a great reader even when I'm staring at a book, so you can imagine what driving by a road sign does to my reading skills, especially when most of the letters are covered in snow.

As we pulled into town and drove down Main Street, a police officer came out of the small, red, brick station and flagged us down. My dad rolled down the window to talk to him.

"Where you folks headed?" the policeman asked.

"New York," my dad told him.

"I'm afraid not today," the officer said. "This storm has closed the road up ahead for the next hundred miles. It's not safe to drive until we get the plows down there, and that's not going to be until tomorrow."

"That's not possible," my dad said. "My wife is having a baby in New York. I have to be there."

"And we have to be there for our mom," I piped up from the backseat. "We're the brother and sister."

"That's tough," said the policeman, shaking his head. I noticed that little icicles were forming on the tips of his reddish brown mustache. "I know how you folks must feel. But the road just isn't safe to drive on."

We were quiet for a moment. This wasn't good. This was terrible. The thought of Mom having a baby without us . . . without our support . . . well, that was just too upsetting to even think about.

We sat there in total silence, except for the small sounds of the snow landing on the hood of the car, the branches rubbing against each other in the wind, and the whistle of a distant train making its way along the tracks.

Wait a minute. Wait just a minute.

Did I hear the whistle of a distant train making its way along the tracks?

Yes, I did.

Thank you ears. You have just saved the day!

CHAPTER
10

I whipped around, faster than you could say "little red caboose," and looked out the back window of the car. Sure enough, there was a train in the distance.

"Does that train stop here?" I asked the police officer.

"You mean right here, where I'm standing?" he said.

Oh, brother! We're in an emergency situation and I get a guy who's a stickler for details.

"No, sir." I tried to sound very patient. "What I meant was . . . does it stop in Belly Ache Falls or Bear Claw Falls . . . or wherever we are, sir."

"That's Bellows Falls, son. And yes, the train's stopped here every day for the past hundred and twenty years."

"Bingo," I said. "That's it, Dad. We'll park

the car here, and hop on the train. It will take us right into New York and we'll be there in plenty of time for the baby. Problem solved."

"Not so fast, son," the policeman said. "That train doesn't go to New York. Its last stop today is Springfield, Massachusetts."

"How far is Springfield?" my dad asked.

"About one hundred miles," he answered.

"That's perfect," Emily commented. "Springfield is located at precisely the mathematical numerical position where the road will re-open."

Emily always finds the hardest way to say anything. It's like if you want to say North Pole, she'll call it "the northernmost point on the Earth's axis." So I wasn't surprised to hear her talking about a mathematical numerical position, whatever that is.

But I'm pretty sure I got her drift. I'm dense on the little points, but most of the time, I can see the big picture.

"I see where you're going with this," I said. "We take the train to Springfield and bypass all the closed roads. Then we'll rent another car or catch a ride from someone and blast into

New York."

"It may not even be snowing there," my dad said.

"That's true," Emily said. "New York City is near the ocean, and everyone knows that the heat-holding ability of large bodies of water causes warming of the air along the coast."

"You got a little scientist there," the officer said to my dad.

"You mean a little show-off," I muttered. I have to confess, it really annoyed me that here I was coming up with a plan to get us home, and Emily was getting the credit for being smart.

My dad reached into his pocket, grabbed his wallet, and took out a handful of bills.

"Here, take this money, run to the station, and buy three tickets," he told us. "Tuck Cheerio in your jacket. I'll park the car on a side street, lock up our luggage and meet you there as fast as I can. Hurry! We can't miss that train."

Emily and I got out of the car and took off running down the main street to the train station. I could see the train pulling into the station, and I hoped we weren't too late.

We burst inside the station, expecting to find

it empty, but to my surprise, there were a lot of people there. Well, a lot of people for Bear Claw Falls or Belly Ache Falls or wherever we were. By that I mean there were about seven people waiting for the train. They all had one thing in common. They were shivering cold.

It wasn't much of a train station. Nothing like Grand Central Station in New York, which is huge and has a giant blue ceiling with all the constellations painted on it. This train station was one small room with three orange, plastic chairs, a vending machine selling hot chocolate and chicken soup, and a grumpy-looking woman sitting behind the glassed-in ticket window.

"I'll buy the tickets," I said to Emily. "You wait over in the corner with Cheerio." I wanted to keep him out of sight, just in case they didn't let dogs on the train.

"Who put you in charge?" Emily asked.

"I did," I informed her. "I'm handling this. After all, I'm the big brother."

Full of confidence, I walked over to the grumpy woman at the ticket window.

"Good afternoon," I said, giving her my best Hank Zipzer smile—the one where I show both my top and bottom teeth. "I'd like three tickets for Springfield please."

I shoved some of the money under the glass window. I am especially terrible at counting money, so I figured I'd just wow her with a handful of bills. She wasn't wowed. In fact, she shoved the money right back at me.

"We're sold out," she said.

"That can't be. We have to get on that train."

"You and every other person who thinks they're going to melt in a little storm," she said. "Everyone's heading south like a flock of scared geese. It's just snow. It's not going to bite you."

"But we have a *real* emergency," I said.

"Can't help you," she said, shaking her head. "All the seats are sold, and fire laws won't allow us to let you stand. End of story, kid."

"My mom's having a baby," I pleaded.

"My mom had one, too," she said. "And it was me."

She gave out a snorty, little laugh, as if her joke was funny. It wasn't to me.

"There must be someplace on that train," I said. "Could we ride with the conductor?"

"Against regulations," she said.

61

"How about the caboose?" I asked.

"Nope. All this train has is two passenger cars, a bunch of coal hoppers, three flatcars carrying lumber from Maine, and a cattle car with horses from upstate heading to Stamford for a horse show."

"You're positive?" I asked.

She didn't even answer this time, just turned her back to me and started typing something on her computer.

Outside on the platform, I heard the screech of brakes and the train pulling to a stop on the platform. Oh no. It was here.

Think, Hank. Think of something!

Suddenly, the station door flew open and my dad came rushing in, his pom-poms flying behind him. He dashed up to me, all out of breath. Little bits of ice had collected on his eyebrows.

"Hank, did you get the tickets?" he asked.

I didn't answer.

"Hank, where are the tickets?" he repeated.

I tried to tell him they were sold out. I opened my mouth to say that. But here's what I said instead: "No problem, Dad. I've got everything under control."

CHAPTER 11

Hank, you're a total moron!

It would have been so much easier to just tell my dad the truth—that there were no more seats on the train. But I didn't. I just couldn't spit it out. It would have made him so upset.

I do this sometimes, and it's not a habit I'm proud of. I open my mouth, dead set on saying the truth, and then *BOOM*, the exact opposite just shoots out like a rocket. Like last week, when my teacher Ms. Adolf asked me if I understood the fractions problem on the board, I wanted to say, "I don't have the slightest clue what those numbers mean." But when I opened my mouth, what came out was, "Are you kidding? I could do that problem in my sleep!" When she asked me to come to the board and solve it, I had to tell her that I thought I had eaten a rotten fish stick at lunch and needed a bathroom pass immediately.

Even though I know that the truth always works out best, I just don't like to disappoint people, and that includes myself. When the truth is hard to say, often it sticks right there in my throat, somewhere between my tonsils and my Adam's apple.

So there I was, leading my Dad and Emily and Cheerio over to the platform where the train was boarding, them thinking everything was all arranged, and me knowing that nothing was arranged. I gave myself one of my typical little smacks in the forehead.

Think fast, brain of mine. It's now or never.

It was as if my dad was reading my mind and knew there was nothing there.

"Give me the tickets, Hank," he said. "I want to check the car number."

"It's okay, Dad. I've got them. They're really special tickets, too."

Special tickets??? Oh, boy. Now I had dug myself in even deeper.

I bolted ahead to the train tracks so I could reach the passenger car first. The conductor was boarding the seven passengers who had been waiting in the station. Luckily, one woman was having a problem with her ticket, and she was in deep conversation with the conductor about whether she was in Seat 3A or 3B.

"We're down this way," I called to my dad and Emily. I turned in the opposite direction of the conductor, walking at a fast pace. I was hoping there was an open door on the other passenger car, and we could just slip in.

No such luck. It turns out the second passenger car was in the opposite direction of where we were walking. We were headed in the direction of the two coal hoppers and the flatcars with the lumber from Maine.

"Hank, are you sure this is right?" Emily called. "These are freight cars."

"Emily, do I look like a guy who doesn't know what he's doing?" I shot back.

"Yes."

"Well, check your eyeballs again, sister. This guy knows where he's going." Why couldn't I just give it up and tell the truth? I was in a pickle, and I don't mean dill.

We walked by the hopper cars and the flatcars. My dad was yelling at me to stop and turn around, but I kept on walking, hoping that an idea would spring into my head. The very last car on the train was a boxcar with open slats along the side. This must have been the one that was filled with horses. When I saw it, I wished I could just jump on one of those horses and ride off into the distance. Then I'd never have to tell my dad the truth about the tickets.

As we walked up to the horse car, I knew it was game over for me. There were no more cars and my dad was insisting we turn around.

"Neeiiigghhhhh!" I heard.

I looked up and saw a pair of dark brown eyes staring out at me from between the slats. They were nice eyes, soft eyes, welcoming eyes.

"Neigh!" the horse said again.

Then he shook his head and snorted as if he were saying, "Hi, Hank. Come on in."

He's inviting us in! There's your answer, Hank! The idea you've been waiting for!

Okay, I know what you're thinking. Horses don't talk. And they don't invite you into their train car for a visit. But I'm telling you, this horse *was* inviting us in. At least, that's what I chose to believe.

CHAPTER 12

I stood in front of the horse car and turned to my Dad and Emily.

"This is our car," I said to them. "Climb in."

"You're kidding me, right?" Emily said.

To show her I wasn't kidding, I jumped up onto the metal step that stood in front of the sliding wood door to the car.

"What are you waiting for?" I asked. "We've got our own personal, private car."

My friend the horse stuck his nose out of the slats and neighed again.

"Well, *almost* private," I added.

"Hank, this is ridiculous!" my dad exclaimed. "We can't ride in a horse car."

"Why not, Dad? It's the best car on the train. Dark, warm, and with a nice horsey smell."

I knew my dad was about to explode, so I

had to act fast. Without waiting for his answer, I slipped off the chain that was holding the door closed and slid the grate open just wide enough for a human to enter. I stepped inside the car.

Wow, I wasn't kidding about the horsey smell!

There weren't any stalls in the car, just ten horses all lined up in a row. They were wearing different colored blankets and were munching on hay that was scattered around the floor. My horse friend was at the end of the row closest to me. When he saw me, he whinnied and pawed the ground. I hoped that was a friendly gesture.

I reached up and patted his neck. I noticed that he was wearing one of those leather strappy things around his face, which I think is called a bridle. Let's assume that's what it's called because I'm pretty sure I'm almost right.

Anyway, his bridle was brown leather, and in gold letters down the side, it said T-R-I-G-G-E-R.

"Is that your name, fella?" I whispered. "Trigger?"

He whinnied again, and nuzzled me right smack in the parka.

"I like you too, Trigger. Now be a good horsey and please . . . stay calm. I'm counting on you."

I reached my hand down to the platform and held it out for Emily.

"Come on, Emily. Trigger here is really friendly, and he wants to meet you."

This was kind of a dirty trick on my part because I know what a sucker Emily is for animals. She gets along better with creatures in the animal kingdom than she does with actual human creatures. The girl even loves iguanas and, trust me, those scaly reptiles are not easy to love.

Emily took my hand and I pulled her up to the metal step. Cheerio, who was in her free arm, got one whiff of the horsey smell drifting out of the train car and started to sneeze and bark at the same time. I don't think he'd ever been that close to a horse, let alone ten horses riding across Massachusetts in an enclosed car.

"Achoo . . . arf . . . achoo . . . arf . . . achooo . . . aaarrfff!"

Man, Cheerio was putting on quite a show.

I was worried that his sneezing attack would freak Trigger out, and then all the horses would follow his lead and start to panic.

"Easy, Trigger," I said, reaching out to pat him again. "Cheerio won't hurt you. He's just having a doggy allergy attack."

Trigger got right up in Cheerio's face and sniffed him up and down. At first I was worried that the horse might have thought Cheerio was a carrot. He is long and narrow and kind of tannish orange. But I didn't have to worry, because after a few sniffs, Trigger stuck his nose under Cheerio's chin and nuzzled him. And not just a little nuzzle either, but a giant, slobbery nuzzle. I think this made the other horses very curious, because within two seconds, they all gathered around Cheerio and started nuzzling him like crazy. Cheerio went limp in Emily's arms and started to purr like a cat. I had never heard him make that noise before.

"How cute is this," Emily said. "They are having an animal group hug."

"It's pretty cool, isn't it?" I nodded.

"Cool, Hank? It's much more than that. This

is Mother Nature at her best. We are witnessing the miracle of inter-species bonding."

The train whistle blew, giving its warning that we were about to pull out of the station any minute.

"Hank and Emily, you come down here right this instant," my dad called up to us.

"It's up to you, Emily. If you can get him up here, you can witness inter-species bonding all the way to Springfield. We'll have a full-fledged nuzzle fest."

I felt a little bad putting the whole responsibility on Emily. But she is much better at convincing my dad to do things than I am. They think alike.

"Dad," Emily said. "We simply have to ride in the horse car. It's important for my education as a scientist. You want me to excel, don't you?"

Education! Scientist! Excel! These words were music to my dad's ears. There is nothing that Stanley Zipzer wants more than an educated, excelling, scientist kid. Unfortunately, that's not me. But hey, I can dance. That's got to count for something.

He climbed up on the metal step and poked his head inside the car.

"Where are we going to sit?" he asked. "This car is completely full of horses."

Suddenly the train jolted ahead, and we were all thrown inside the car. We had to hang on to the slats so we didn't fall down.

"Great, Hank," my dad said, as the train picked up speed and pulled out of the station. "Now it's too late to change cars and use our real tickets."

"Oh well," I said. "Who wants to ride in a stupid passenger car, anyway? It's so dull and ordinary . . ."

"And warm," my dad shivered. "We have to get away from these open slats. Let's huddle up in the center of the car."

We tried to find our way to the center, but trust me, ten horses take up a whole lot of room and there wasn't any left for us. We were standing pressed right up against them, toe-to-hoof, hoof-to-toe.

"Stop tickling me when I'm trying to find a place to stand, Hank," Emily said. "That's so immature."

"I'm not tickling you," I told her. "He is."

Emily turned her head around and saw that Trigger's tail was swishing along the back of her neck. As much as she likes animals, I don't think she liked that much. We barely had room to breathe.

"Can I make a suggestion?" I said. "Instead of standing BEHIND the horses or wedging in BETWEEN the horses, why don't we sit ON the horses? I mean, isn't that what people do?"

I used the slats of the car like a ladder and was able to climb aboard Trigger. He didn't seem to mind me sitting on him one bit. Emily handed Cheerio up to me, then did exactly as I had done, and climbed on the back of the horse next to me. I could see from his bridle that his name was Hopalong. The horse on the other side of me was named Silver.

"Come on up, Dad. Silver is waiting for you."

And then . . . Stanley Zipzer, worker of crossword puzzles, programmer of computers, and all around couch potato, suddenly threw his leg over Silver's back and jumped up on that horse like he was the Lone Ranger.

"Hi ho, Silver," he said. "Yee haw."

"Are you okay, Dad?"

"I'm worried about your mother and the baby," he said. "I just need to release a little pressure."

Then, out of the blue, he began to sing a big-time cowboy version of "Home on the Range." I mean with yodeling and whooping and hollering and everything. In fact, he kept singing it all the way to Springfield. He must have had a lot of pressure to release.

That, along with the nuzzle fest to end all nuzzle fests, made the next two hours on the train two of the more interesting hours in my life. Weird, but definitely interesting.

Wait until I tell the new baby brother about this, I kept thinking. *He's going to want to go right back where he came from.*

CHAPTER 13

TEN THINGS I WAS SURE TRIGGER WAS THINKING ABOUT US

1. About that guy in the striped zebra pants . . . where are his other two legs?
2. And those red, round things hanging off his hat, those are the smallest hairy apples I've ever seen.
3. If that old guy doesn't stop singing that song, I'm going to buck him through the door.
4. Will somebody please tell this Hank kid to get his heels out of my side? My flanks are killing me.
5. Oh, look. There's a cow standing outside in the snow. "Hey, moo face, ever heard of a barn?"
6. Hey . . . there's a whole herd of them,

standing around chewing their cud, freezing their hooves off. I feel sorry for them—just a bunch of horse wannabes.

7. Aww, look at that cute, little carrot dog. He looks like he could use another nuzzle.

8. Oh wait. The girl with the pig tails wants a nuzzle, too. Funny, she smells a little like an iguana.

9. The old guy's still singing. "Hey, Hopalong, let's all turn around and stare at him. Maybe we can scare him into stopping."

10. I got an itch on my hind quarters. Hey kid, why don't you make yourself useful and scratch it. Just my luck . . . he doesn't understand horse.

11. How much longer do I have to stay up here on this thing . . . my butt's falling asleep. *Oh, wait . . . that's not Trigger's thought . . . that's mine.*

CHAPTER 14

After about two hours in the horse car, we were more than ready to get off in Springfield. We said good-bye to Trigger and Hopalong and Silver, and I apologized to them for not having any carrots or apples. The best part was we managed to get off the train without the conductor seeing us, so I didn't have to confess that I never got the tickets. Let's keep it our secret, okay? I mean, if Emily knew a thing like that, she'd bring it up every day until I'm sixty.

We headed through the empty station. No one was there. They must have all gone home to sit by the fireplace, and I couldn't blame them. It was cold. And to make things even more uncomfortable, we were walking like we each had a barrel stuck between our legs. I felt muscles I didn't even know were in my body. If I had to pick one word to describe my thighs, it would be like having a really bad headache in your legs . . . which is way more than one word, but I think makes an excellent point.

So there we were, at the entrance to the train station in Springfield, Massachusetts. We looked out the glass front doors, and all we could see was a blanket of white. There wasn't one detail of the landscape that you could recognize. There was one tall, pointy, white thing, which could either have been the church steeple, a flagpole, or a rocket launching pad. Now that I think about it, I've never heard of a rocket taking off from Massachusetts.

As if it wasn't bad enough to be stuck in a train station with no trains in the middle of a giant, and I mean humongous, blizzard, Emily picked that moment to totally flip out.

"I'm starving," she said. "My stomach is growling like a lion and I can't take it anymore. I need energy to move forward."

"No problem, Emily. I happen to have a turkey and Swiss on rye, with extra mayo, just the way you like it," I offered.

"Really, Hank?"

"No, of course not really. Do you see a

sandwich shop that happens to be open? No. But I do have right here in my pocket three gummy bears and a cherry lifesaver. Okay, they have frozen together into a sculpture but it would be my pleasure to let you have them."

I held out the gummy mess in my mitten and shoved it in Emily's direction. She was not grateful.

Oh no. I thought I saw those tears brimming up in her beady eyes again.

"You start to cry and those tears are going to freeze to your cheek," I warned her. "And if that happens, then we'll have to . . . well, you don't even want to know what the next steps are."

At that very moment, my dad let out a sound I've never heard before. If a voice could jump up and down with excitement, that's what his throat was doing. Poor Cheerio. The sound made his ears stand at attention, and it was so cold in that station, they never flopped down again.

"Look!" my father finally managed to say.

He pointed through the door of the train station to the road beyond. Coming toward us were two yellow circles, giving off an eerie kind of light in the snowy mist. Either it was a man-eating monster alien looking for fresh families to devour, or it was a truck. Knowing that it was too cold for any sane man-eating monster alien to be out and about, I decided it had to be a truck.

"We're not alone!" my dad croaked out.

Without saying another word to each other, we all raced through the door.

The lights kept getting closer. We waved our arms like maniacs to make sure they wouldn't miss us. Or hit us.

"It's slowing down," I tried to say through my chattering teeth. "They see us!"

Cheerio buried his face in my parka. I think his little teeth were chattering, too.

As the truck slid to a stop right next to us, we were able to see the letters on the side of it. It said, "Krinkle Krispy Doughnuts, New England's Dunkin' Best."

"You see, I am a good person," Emily said. "They stopped just for me, to bring me doughnuts."

"You're nuts," I said to her. "You think this truck is cruising around in the snow, looking for hungry reptile lovers?"

"Maybe," said Emily, unwilling to lose her ridiculous argument. "Anyway, I'm going to eat everything in that whole truck."

"Could you just save Dad and me one?" I asked. "And maybe a doughnut hole for Cheerio."

Emily was so out of control with hunger that she didn't even wait for the driver to roll down the window. She jumped up on the running board and started pounding on the door. When the door opened and the driver stuck his head out, Emily took one look at him, screamed at the top of her lungs, and fell backward in the snow.

He was half man, half dragon. Or at least, that's the way he looked. His entire face was painted red, except for the area around his eyes, which was green with fish scales. His fingernails were silver and pointed and when he smiled, his teeth were as yellow as the lights on his truck.

I didn't know what this dragon man was doing driving on a totally empty road in a blizzard, but I did know one thing. He didn't seem like the type of guy who would hand out free doughnuts.

CHAPTER 15

Emily sprang to her feet, pivoted like an NBA player, and took off into the snow, screaming, "Run for your life!"

When I looked over at the guy, he seemed to be smiling in a warm, friendly kind of way. And when Cheerio stuck his nose out of my parka and looked at him, his tail started to wag. Cheerio has a very good sense about people. When he likes you, you're usually an okay kind of person. Except for our pizza delivery guy. I don't know what it is about him, but every time we open the door for him, Cheerio takes his attack dog position and barks like a German shepherd. No offense to Cheerio, but he's not too scary even when he's trying his hardest.

"Wait up, Emily," I called after her. "Maybe this guy can help us." I looked over at my dad, who was checking the guy out pretty carefully.

"What do you say, Dad?"

"Let me speak to him," my dad said. "I believe this man is some kind of stage performer."

"Good afternoon, sir," my dad said to the dragon guy. "We have an emergency here, and we're in need of your assistance. We have to get to New York City. Are you, by any chance, going in that direction?"

"*Ni hao*," the man said to my dad.

"I can't believe this," Emily said, coming out from behind the bus stop where she had been hiding. "We stopped the only person in all of Massachusetts who doesn't speak English." Then she did a very un-Emily like thing. Cupping her hands around her mouth, she started to yell.

"Help! Help!" she cried. "Is there a translator around who just happens to speak Chinese?"

"I do," I said.

"This is no time to joke around, Hank."

"I'm not joking. The guy said hello. *Ni hao* means 'hello.'"

"You speak Chinese?" she asked, her mouth hanging open.

"Well not the whole language. Ashley taught

me to say hello, and also *wo hen gao xin*, which means 'I am happy.'"

When the dragon man heard me say that, he flashed me a really friendly smile and said, "*Ni leng ma?*"

Unfortunately, that wasn't a phrase Ashley taught me, so I just smiled and nodded as if I understood. He smiled and nodded right back at me. He was a nice guy, and whatever it was I agreed to seemed to please him.

"Since this man doesn't understand our language," my dad said, "I am going to use the universal language of the body. Watch how this is done, kids. First I wave my hands in the air to get his attention."

My dad stood by the window of the truck and waved his hands around like he was erasing an imaginary blackboard. The man must have thought this was fun, because he started doing exactly the same thing. Then he turned around and said something to someone in the back of the truck. All of a sudden, the two back doors of the van flew open and at least nine men and women in dragon makeup and colorful silk robes came flying out. They formed a semi-circle around us and all started erasing the same imaginary blackboard.

Cheerio thought this was tremendously fun, and started thrashing his tail with happiness. With every wag, he flipped snow up in the air. Thank goodness I had my thick parka on, because without it, his tail thrashing would have made my rib area completely black and blue.

The blackboard erasing dance went on for a long time.

"Dad, this is getting mind-bogglingly weird," I whispered.

"I'm feeling no danger signal whatsoever," my dad said. "These people are clearly a traveling circus troop of some kind. We just have to communicate our need to them."

With that, my dad stepped forward, took a bow, and went into a pantomime that I can only describe as a hippopotamus trying to do ballet. Remember, he was wearing his zebra-striped ski pants and his red and white hat with the pom-poms, so his look was pretty eccentric to begin with. Add in some of his hippo moves, and his pantomime became one of the stranger sights anyone could ever hope to see.

"Me," my dad said, pointing to himself and kind of pounding on his chest.

"And my children," he said, grabbing Emily and me and pointing to us like we were bear cubs in a zoo.

"And our family dog," he pointed to Cheerio and made a barking sound that set off a barking fit in Cheerio.

"We all have to get to my wife," he said, pulling off his ski glove and pointing to his wedding ring.

It wasn't working. All ten of the acrobats were doing exactly what our dad was doing—pounding on their chest, patting us on the head, and pointing to their ring finger, whether they had a wedding ring or not.

In any other circumstance, this game of charades might have been a lot of fun, but we were way too cold for fun. We were sounding like a symphony of chattering teeth out there. This was definitely not the right temperature for a game of charades.

"Excuse me, Dad. Maybe I can speed this up a bit," I said.

Without waiting for his answer, I handed

Cheerio to Emily, stepped in front of good old Stanley, and did what I considered to be an excellent pantomime of someone driving a truck. I even shifted gears, just to make sure they got the point.

"Can you drive us to New York?" I said, continuing to mime driving the truck.

Nine of the acrobats imitated me, laughing and shifting and steering up a storm, which by the way, we were already in. However, the driver and I made contact, and by that, I mean brain-to-brain contact. He understood me. I could almost see the light go on in his head.

"Ahhhhhhhhhhh," he said. Then he said something which sounded a lot like "New York." Okay, it sounded kind of like New York. Well, at least a little bit like it.

"See, Dad, they're going to New York," I said.

The driver got a big smile on his face, and started to mime something back at me. Using his thumb, he jerked it toward the back of the truck, which could only mean one thing.

GET IN.

You didn't have to ask me twice.

"They're going to give us a ride," I said to

my dad and Emily. "Come on."

Before we could even move, three of the acrobats grabbed our hands and led us to the back of the truck. Another one gently took Cheerio from Emily's arms and carried him. Cheerio liked the guy immediately, and started licking his face. I noticed that he got a little of the guy's green makeup on his tongue, giving him a slightly iguana look. He was a whole lot cuter than Katherine.

The other acrobats clustered around, as if to protect us or keep us warm. The driver got out of the car and came up to us. He pointed at himself.

"Chin," he said.

I thought maybe he wanted to learn English.

"No," I said, pointing at my chin. "This is a chin."

He shook his head back at me, and pointed to himself again.

"Chin," he repeated.

"Chin," I said, pointing to my chin.

"You are such a moron, Hank," Emily said. "His name is Chin. Can't you see that's what he's telling you?"

I hate it when Emily's right, but I had to admit, my brain had kind of misfired on that one.

"Oooohhhh," I said to him. "*Ni hao*, Mr. Chin."

He smiled, then gestured us into the back of the truck. He went right to work, clearing off the snow that had accumulated on the windshield during our mime-a-thon.

When we looked in the back door of the van, the first thing out of Emily's mouth was, "No way."

"Yes, way," I said. "Get in."

"There's no way the nine of them and the three of us and Cheerio will fit inside there," she said. "It's simple math, Hank."

"First of all, Emily, math is never simple. And second of all, be quiet and get in."

"Stop bickering, kids," my dad said. "Mr. Chin and his troop are being kind, so let's not air our dirty family laundry in front of them."

I don't know what a bunch of dirty socks and boxers had to do with our situation, but Emily and I could tell from my dad's tone of voice that he meant business. So we cut our argument short and started to climb inside the back of the mini-truck. But just before we could get in, a surprising thing happened. I mean, extremely surprising.

One of the acrobats tapped me on the shoulder and motioned for me to step aside. Then, he did a back flip right by me, and catapulted himself into the van. Once inside, he got on his hands and knees and scrunched himself up against the front seat where the driver was getting into his seat. Then he whistled, and three more acrobats somersaulted by us and landed inside the truck. They also got on their hands and knees and scrunched into a row on either side of the first guy.

"What do you think is going on?" Emily asked.

"I don't know," I said, "but they're so good, they could charge admission."

With that, the first guy whistled again and two of the women acrobats whizzed by us, jumping into the van and flipping on the backs of the four guys who were crouched inside.

"Look at that," I said. "They're making a human pyramid."

"Great, Hank," Emily said. "And while they're horsing around, I've just become a human icicle."

"They're not horsing around, Emily, they're . . ."

Before I was able to finish that sentence, the next two acrobats, who were smaller than the others, somersaulted by us into the van. They folded themselves up into a very compact shape and sat down on either side of the pyramid. I'm not sure what happened to their arms and legs, but they somehow folded up next to them like Papa Pete's old coffee table.

One acrobat was left standing next to us. I wondered what he was going to do, but I didn't have to wonder long.

Whoosh! He zoomed by me, jumped into the truck, and sat down cross-legged in between the two coffee tables. Then he grabbed one leg and put it behind his ear. But wait, that's not all. He grabbed his other leg, and put it behind the other ear. And if that wasn't enough, he took each of his arms and threaded them through the holes his legs created.

And there he was, a human pretzel.

"That's got to hurt," I said to Emily.

"I sure hope they're not expecting us to become bendable buddies," Emily said.

"Look what they've done, kids," my dad said. "They've created enough room for the three of us and Cheerio."

And so we got in.

"Thank you very much," I said to the acrobats.

They just looked at me, and I realized that of course, they didn't know what I was saying. So I used both hands to pat my heart. Emily and my dad did the same.

"Ahhhhhhhh," they all said at once. And then they used one hand to pat their hearts, too. Everybody except the guy who made himself into a pretzel. He patted some part of his body, but I'm not sure what it was. I think it was his ankle but it could have been his nose.

The truck took off, bumping along on the snowy road.

This certainly wasn't the fastest way any-one ever got to New York, but it was the most unusual.

CHAPTER 16

TEN USEFUL THINGS YOU NEED TO KNOW WHEN YOU'RE STUFFED IN THE BACK OF A VAN LIKE A SAUSAGE WITH NINE CHINESE ACROBATS

1. Really nothing, because the chances of you ever being stuffed in the back of a van with a human pyramid, two human coffee tables, and a human pretzel are slim to none. So, I've decided to blow off this list and substitute it with the ten things that flew into my imagination as we bumped along the snowy road . . . slowly.

THE NEW LIST

1. If they built a bathroom in the back of this van, where would they put it? And boy, could I use it!
2. I wish I hadn't given those old gummy bears

93

with the lifesaver frozen on them to Emily, because I would eat them right now.

3. I wish this was really a doughnut truck.

4. If it were, I'd get the classic glazed, or no wait, maybe a jelly-filled one with chocolate sprinkles on the top. No wait, a lemon cream with powdered sugar.

5. I hope my mom is okay and that there wasn't a long line when she checked into the hospital. She hates lines even two people long.

6. I hope there's a hot chocolate machine on her floor, for her and for me.

7. I wonder if Emily's butt is still numb from the cold. Actually, I don't want to wonder that. *Thought, get out of my brain right now.*

8. I wonder if babies have eyelashes when they're born.

9. Note to self: When I grow up, never wear a ski hat with red pom-poms. That is a big no-no.

10. These guys should go in the Guinness Book of World Records for holding an uncomfortable position for the longest time ever. It's amazing that they did this for us.

11. Whoops. Did someone fart?

CHAPTER 17

There were two great things about being in that van. The first was HEAT. It must have been negative two hundred degrees out there in the snow. The driver had the heater blasting, plus there was the heat that thirteen bodies and a dachshund make when they're jammed together like M&M's in a bag. The second great thing was that the acrobats had food. It wasn't doughnuts, like I had hoped, or a peanut butter and jelly sandwich, but it was food and with the way our stomachs were growling, I would have eaten a shoe.

The acrobats must have known how hungry we were. Actually, it wasn't that hard to tell if your ears were working. When Emily's stomach and mine growl, it sounds kind of normal. But when my dad is hungry, his stomach sounds like a locomotive.

Anyway, the first acrobat at the bottom of the pyramid, using one hand to balance himself, reached out his other hand into his neighbor's coat pocket and pulled out what looked like a power bar covered with sesame seeds. He passed it over to us, and gestured that we should help ourselves to it. I ripped the wrapper off, took a bite, and passed it to Emily. She took two bites, because she was really starving, and passed what was left to my dad, who popped the whole thing into his mouth. I have to say, it didn't make a dent in my hunger. My stomach growled again.

So the middle guy on the bottom of the pyramid balanced on one hand and reached into his neighbor's pocket and pulled out a banana. Now we were talking real food. He passed it over to me, and this time, I broke it into equal thirds. (Did you notice I'm getting a little better with my fractions?)

Cheerio, who had been asleep under one of the human coffee tables, got a whiff of the banana, and suddenly came to life. His tail started to wag at top speed, which is danger-ous when you're shoved into the back of a van like a jar of pickles. His little tail was whipping all of us. I mean, there wasn't one of us he missed, except for the two guys on the top of the pyramid.

"Easy, boy," I said to him.

But he wasn't about to calm down until he chowed down. One of the guys on the top row reached into his neighbor's pocket and pulled out a piece of beef jerky. Wow, these guys were like a human grocery store. The guy tossed it toward Cheerio, and when Cheerio smelled it, he flew through the air like a doggy acrobat. I think he really impressed everybody, because they all cheered. Cheerio really liked that, because I think I saw him smile.

The acrobats continued to pull treats out of each other's pockets. Let's see. There was another banana; a sticky taffy candy; a fishy tasting, dried thing I don't even want to think about; an almond cookie; and a couple of other tastes I couldn't identify. Finally, our stomachs went silent.

After the meal, I was feeling happier, and as we drove along the snowy highway, I start-ed to hum a little song, one of the songs my mom always sings when we're on a road trip. It's kind of a stupid little song called "She'll Be Coming 'Round the Mountain." It made me think of my mom all alone in the hospital. I hoped she wasn't sacred.

Then, one by one, the acrobats joined in singing! I mean, they knew the words. So here we were, in the middle of somewhere in Massachusetts or maybe Connecticut, in a blinding snowstorm, singing, like a choir. I know you're not going to believe this, but trust me, I'm telling you it happened. And it sounded beautiful.

However, there's only so long you can sing "She'll be Coming 'Round the Mountain" when you're worried. After more than an hour of driving, my dad started checking his watch, and I mean checking . . . like every six seconds. Then he started that throat-clearing noise like he does when he can't come up with the right crossword puzzle word. It's the kind of noise you make when you're just clearing your throat for the fun of it. You know, when there's nothing to clear.

"Hank, can you see out the window?" he asked me, clearing his throat as he talked. "I want to make sure we're still going in the right direction."

I tried getting up to my knees to get a glimpse out the window, but I couldn't see past the second row of the human pyramid.

"No, Dad. All I see are the tops of heads and the bottoms of feet."

"We should be well into Connecticut by now," he said. "Look for a road sign."

I tried again, but this time all I got was nine pairs of eyes looking back at me.

"No luck, Dad."

"I really need to know where we are," he said. "I want to figure out our E.T.A."

E.T.A. What is he talking about? Eating Table Attitude. No, that doesn't make sense. Entering Tunnel Approach? Maybe, but I never heard of that before. I got it! Eat Turnips, America! Whoops, now I'm really lost.

"What's an E.T.A., Dad?" I hated to bother him with definitions at a time like this, but as you can see, I hadn't come up with much on my own.

"Estimated time of arrival," he said.

Wow, I would never have figured that out in

a million years.

I could tell he couldn't stand the tension anymore, because all of a sudden, he popped up and started to make his way toward the front of the van. This was definitely not a good idea, or an easy one, because he had to snake his way around the clump of bodies that formed the wall of the pyramid. And don't forget the human pretzel who was still there twisted up in a knot.

Stanley Zipzer is not a small man, or a particularly graceful one, so this was quite an operation. As he made his way over to the window, there was a lot of grunting on his part, and a lot of laughing on the acrobats' parts. But he finally made it to the front, so he could peer over the seat and look out the windshield.

"All I see is snow," he said. "It's just a blanket of white everywhere. Will it ever end?"

"Did you know that in the United States, a typical snowstorm will have a snow producing lifetime of two to five days?" Emily piped up.

"That's my Emily," I said. "Always there with the helpful info . . . that doesn't help us at all at this moment."

"It's science, Hank. Live with it."

"Enough of that, kids," my dad said. "I'm trying to concentrate and see where we are."

He stared out the window for a long time, as if staring would make him see better or make the snow disappear. I felt really bad for him. My mom was counting on him to be there. She had been saying that for months. And now he couldn't be there. That must have felt awful for him. I know, because it felt awful for me, too.

And then an amazing thing happened. Well, it's not actually so amazing that it would make the ten most amazing things list. But to us, at that moment, it was totally amazing. Like a magic trick, a sign appeared on the highway, lit up in red digital letters. It was a marvelous sight to see, this beautiful, red sign floating in whiteness all around us.

And here's what it said:

ENTERING NEW HAVEN, CONNECTICUT

NEW YORK: 80 MILES

Eighty miles.

Wow. That seemed close. We were actually going to get there!

Or so I thought.

CHAPTER 18

My dad reached behind him, grabbed my shoulder, and gave me a hearty squeeze. If you ask me, it was a little too hearty, but I could understand that this was an exciting moment for him.

"New York," he said. "We're almost home, Hank."

"It's still eighty miles, Dad," Emily pointed out. "So close, and yet so far away."

"Emily, could you think positive for once in your life?" I asked her. "We could still be on that mountaintop in Vermont, with you whimpering like a scared rabbit."

"Rabbits are silent, Hank. They do not employ their vocal chords unless they're in extreme danger."

"Why don't you follow their example, then? You could learn a thing or two from a bunny."

Emily and I were so busy arguing, that we didn't notice the van slowing down. But my dad did.

"What's going on?" he asked the driver, who, of course, didn't understand a word he was saying.

My dad just started pointing like a mad man at the sign that said New York.

"That's where we're going," he kept saying. "New York. Please, we have to get there."

The dragon man just smiled at him and nodded his head. He also continued to slow down and pull over to the side of the road.

"New York," my dad said. "Please."

The car was stopped now, and the driver just looked at my dad without understanding. In desperation, my dad tried to say please in every other language he knew.

"Por favor," he tried in Spanish.

"Bitte," he said in German.

"S'il vous plait," he tried in French.

"Grzyb," he tried in whatever language that was.

"What are you speaking now, Dad?" I asked.

"Polish," he said.

"I didn't know you knew how to say please in Polish."

"I don't," he said. "I said mushroom."

"Wow, you must be really stressed, Dad. Calm down for a minute and let me give it a try."

So now it was mime time again. I crawled over the pyramid until I was facing the driver. In slow motion, I acted out each word.

"We," I said, pointing to myself.

"Are going," I said, pointing to the sign, "to New York."

The dragon man watched me carefully, trying to understand. When he repeated what I had just said, this time it didn't sound like he was saying New York at all. It was New Something... but definitely not New York.

Uh-oh.

"My mother," I went on, "is having a baby." With that, I grabbed the driver's hat from the seat and stuffed it under my parka so I looked pregnant. Well, at least kind of pregnant. Then I picked up an imaginary baby and rocked it in my arms.

"Baby," I said. And just to make sure it was all clear, I repeated, "Baby in New York." As a finishing touch, I started to cry like a baby.

"Waaahhhhhh," I cried. "Waaaaaahhhhh in New York."

The driver was silent for a minute, putting together all my mime clues. Then suddenly it hit him.

"Aahhhhhh," he said. Then he handed me a piece of paper with a lot of writing on it. The letters were so small and so close together, I couldn't focus on them. The whole page was a blur, so I handed it as quickly as I could to my dad.

"The driver wants us to see this," I said.

"Mr. Chin and His Amazing Acrobats of Cheng Du," he read.

"That must be these guys," Emily said. "So they're not doughnut bakers."

"Duh," I said to her. She stuck her tongue out at me.

"You look just like your ugly iguana when you do that," I said.

"Katherine is not ugly. She's quite attractive, in my opinion."

"Kids," my father said. "Not now. Listen to this. Mr. Chin and His Amazing Acrobats of Cheng Du are appearing Saturday evening at Shubert Theater in New Haven, Connecticut. What day is today?"

"Saturday," I said. "That's tonight, Dad."

"No wonder they stopped the van," my dad said. "They're not going to New York. They're turning off the main road here. To New Haven."

So that's what the dragon man was saying. Not New York. New Haven.

Now it was our turn to say, "Oohhhhhhhh."

And all three of our heads dropped at the same time. We were stuck, still eighty miles from New York, and there wasn't another car in sight. How were we going to get out of this pickle? I was completely out of ideas. I mean, my brain was shut down tight. I closed my eyes really tight and tried to squeeze them as hard as I could to start my brain thinking. But all that happened was nothing. A whole lot of nothing.

I hit my forehead with the palm of my hand, trying to knock a thought loose. It must have worked because suddenly I had an idea.

"Hey, Dad," I said. "Give me your cell phone."

He handed me the phone, and I checked the battery. It was low, but maybe I had enough juice left to make a call. Maybe.

I dialed the number and waited.

CHAPTER 19

THE TWELVE THINGS I SAID ON THE PHONE

1. Hey, Frankie. It's Hank.
2. Frankie!!! Frankie??? It's Hank.
3. I can't hear you, either.
4. I still can't hear you.
5. How's my mom?
6. No, Frankie. *My* mom. Not *your* mom.
7. Excuse me, Mr. Pretzel Man. Can you take your foot out from behind your ear?
8. No, Frankie. Not *your* foot. One of the Chin guys' foot. No, not his *chin*. His foot. It's behind his *ear*.
9. No, not his *rear*. His *ear*.
10. Tell your mom to tell my mom that . . . What? You're breaking up.
11. Frankie? Frankie!!! Frankie????
12. *Click*. Dial tone. Nothing.

CHAPTER 20

I was so frustrated that I slammed the phone shut and just sat there, staring at Mr. Chin. He smiled at me and said something in Chinese that I didn't understand. Sure, easy for him to smile. He was on his way to New Haven to twist himself up like a rubber band. We, on the other hand, had to get out of the van and get back into the snowstorm with no hope of making the final leg into New York. I could only imagine what kind of fit Emily was going to throw when her toes started to freeze up again.

Suddenly, out of the corner of my eye, I saw a pack of dogs approaching us—all different kinds of dogs. The first dog looked like a husky, one of those dogs that pulls dogsleds. He was surrounded by a boxer, a golden retriever, a labrador, a poodle, and another fluffy dog that looked like a shaggy rug covered in snow. For a minute, I thought they were lost dogs looking for shelter.

But then I realized that the dogs weren't alone, because right in back of them was a sled. And on that sled was a guy, standing up and guiding the dogs along the road. Whoa . . . a dogsled! Had we taken a wrong turn to Alaska? Once I saw a documentary on the Discovery Channel about people who race dogsleds for thousands of miles across snow and frozen lakes and glaciers and everything. Hey, if they could do that, maybe this guy could find his way to New York. With us aboard, naturally.

As soon as that thought hit my mind, I reached over Mr. Chin's shoulder and started honking the horn like a nutcase.

"Hey," I shouted at the top of my voice, as Mr. Chin rolled down the window. "Where are you headed?"

When the dogs heard the horn honking, they stopped dead in their tracks, turned, and stared at us.

This was great. I was sure they were waiting to hear what I had in mind. But before I could even open the door to get out of the van, the dogs suddenly took off, running like they were chasing an imaginary tennis ball that had to be yellow so they could see it in the snow.

"Hey, come back here!" I hollered out the window. "We need a ride. It's an emergency."

Cheerio must have heard the dogs barking because his ears perked up and started to twitch. He's a pretty social little guy, and there's nothing he likes better than a pack of neighborhood dogs he hasn't met before. He loves making new friends. With his stubby little legs, he climbed over the acrobats and jumped into the front seat and onto Mr. Chin's lap. Sticking his head out the window, he barked his version of "Hey, guys. Come on back. Let's have a cup of hot chocolate."

I don't speak dog, but I'm sure that's what he meant.

When the pack of dogs heard his invitation, they did a U-turn and came charging directly toward the truck. It was hard to see through the falling snow, but I think the driver almost fell off the sled. All the dogs were attached to one main leash, and although he was holding on to it, it sure looked to me like the dogs were in control of the sled.

When the sled pulled up to the van, Cheerio stuck his head out the window and started talking to the pack of dogs, making little howling sounds. It sounded just like he was saying hello. They couldn't answer him because they were panting so hard. There was enough steam coming out of their mouths to boil an egg. But I could tell they were happy to see him, because their tails were wagging like crazy.

I shivered. Six tails wagging creates a wind gust, and it was all coming in our direction.

The driver got off the sled and came over to the window. He was wearing about ten jackets. He looked like he had swallowed a tuba. His arms were so padded, they practically stuck straight out from his body.

"Are you guys stuck?" he said. "It's a heck of a day for a drive."

As he lowered his eyes to the window and caught sight of Mr. Chin, he stopped talking.

"Hey, buddy, Halloween was four months ago. What's with the dragon face?"

Mr. Chin had no idea what the guy was saying. He just had a smile plastered on his face.

I could see the back doors of the van opening, and my dad climbing out to come talk to this guy, but in the meantime, I thought I'd keep up my end of the conversation.

"These nice folks are a traveling acrobatic group from China," I said to the sled driver.

Cheerio yipped in agreement.

"And this is our dog Cheerio. I'm Hank Zipzer. My sister Emily is in the back with my dad Stanley."

The sled driver cut me short.

"It's pretty cold standing here," he said. "How many more in your family?"

"There's my mom," I said. "But she's not here right now. She's in New York having a new baby and we have to get there right away."

"So Mr. Dragon here is taking you?"

"That's the problem," I said. "Mr. Chin and his troop are staying here in New Haven. Are you heading to New York, by any chance?"

"I'm going as far as the Bronx. I have to pick up a fuel pump for my snowplow. It broke down just when the storm hit and it's got to be fixed by morning so I can clear the roads for the supermarket to open."

That explained why he was out in a dogsled in the middle of a snowstorm. I didn't think it was just for a joy ride.

"Do you have room for three more in your sled?" I asked him.

Cheerio gave another one of his yips, which, I'm sure, in dog talk meant: "Please say yes."

"I don't know. That's a lot of weight for the dogs to pull."

"Cheerio can help," I said.

The driver shot a look at Cheerio. "Looks like he couldn't pull a box of pencils," he said. "No offense intended."

"None taken. He's much stronger than he looks," I told the driver.

Cheerio yipped again, three times. I'll bet he was trying to say, "I was born to pull a sled."

By this time, my dad had reached the driver. It took him a while because for each step he took, he had to pull his leg out of the thigh-high snow.

"Dad," I said. "This man . . . I'm sorry . . . what was your name?"

"Harley," he said. "Harley Obama. No relation, unfortunately."

"Harley here is going to the Bronx."

"That's still a half an hour away from the hospital," my dad pointed out.

"But it's a lot closer than where we are now," Emily piped up from the seat behind me.

"Good thinking, Emily," my dad said. Emily! What kind of thinking did she do? I'm the one who asked Harley for a ride!

For my mom's sake, I decided to ignore that and just keep my mouth shut, which believe me, is not used to being shut.

"Harley," my dad said. "If you could give us a lift, I'd be more than happy to buy you a bag of dog food . . . instead of gas."

"That's not necessary, sir," Harley said. "Just name the baby after me."

We all laughed, but I thought, *Harley Obama Zipzer. The kid could do worse.*

So it was settled. Emily, my dad, and I would ride on the sled with Harley. And Cheerio would help pull. While Harley was tying Cheerio up to the leash next to the little poodle, I thought how strange the whole day had been. Wow, this was turning out to be the adventure of a lifetime.

I sure hoped my mom was hanging in there.

CHAPTER 21

We said a big thank you and a warm good-bye to Mr. Chin and his traveling troop. As I climbed out of the van, I noticed that all the acrobats in the back were unfolding themselves. The coffee table, the pretzel, and the pyramid turned back into nine separate people. Boy, that must have felt great for them. It was really cool of them to be that uncomfortable for that long, just to help us get to that new baby who was going to poop and spew all over my room.

We stood there and waved good-bye to the van as it took off toward New Haven. Then we turned our attention to New York.

"How long do you think it will take us to get to the city?" my dad asked Harley.

"Well, there's no traffic because everyone's off the road in this storm," he said. "So we should be able to mush along at a good clip.

Providing the dogs don't have to take too many pit stops."

"So in mush terms, how long are we talking?" my dad asked.

"Maybe two hours, give or take."

"Two hours!" Emily said. "I'm going to freeze."

"Don't worry, little lady," Harley said. "I brought along an extra coat, but it wouldn't fit over the ten I've got on already. You can wrap yourself up in it like a blanket."

Harley adjusted the leash to make sure Cheerio was comfortable. Cheerio seemed really happy to be in the pack. That's because he had no idea what was about to happen. Poor little guy, he thought he was at a puppy party. Little did he know that his legs were going to run like they've never run before.

We climbed into the sled, and Harley stood in back of us, holding the leash.

"Mush," he yelled.

All the dogs knew what to do, except Cheerio, and boy did he learn fast. They took off running along the road, with the husky in the lead. Cheerio had no choice but to keep

117

up, running along the tracks made by the two dogs in front of him. If he veered off even a few inches, he would be lost in the deep snow. He was running next to the little poodle, who was named Claude-Pierre. Harley told us that the lead dog was named Linus. The others were Dexter, Raymond, Poopsie (I think you can guess why), and Mr. Winterbottom.

And I thought Cheerio was a weird name.

We slid along the road at a pretty good pace. Emily wrapped herself up in Harley's coat so all you could see were her eyes peeking above the collar. My dad's pom-poms were flying in the breeze behind him, and they kept hitting Harley in the face, but he was such a nice guy, he didn't complain. I sat in front, looking out for bumps in the road. Every now and then, I'd call a warning out to Harley.

"Ice patch up ahead!" or "Stalled car off to the right!"

I'm pretty sure it was the right, but knowing me, it could have been the left.

Before we had gone very far, the sled started to slow down. Harley pulled on the leash and yelled, "Whoa, doggies!"

"Why are we stopping?" my dad asked him.

"Your little wiener dog isn't cutting it," he said. "He's not pulling his weight."

"Hey, he's trying his best," I said.

"Remember," Emily added, "all four of his legs barely equal one of Linus's."

I had to hand it to her. Her math skills certainly came in handy.

"Can't you give him one more chance?" I asked. "It will make him feel so bad about himself to be taken out of the line. It's embarrassing. Trust me. I really know that feeling."

"This is no time for doggy sensitivity training," Harley told me. "We've got to make good time, and he's holding us back."

"He's right, Hank," my dad agreed. "Harley's got to get his fuel pump, and we have to get to the hospital as fast as we can."

I gave in. "Okay. But let me break the news to Cheerio."

I got out of the sled, went up to Cheerio, and kneeled down next to him in the snow. The first thing he did was lick my face. That made matters worse, because now I was going to have to tell him the bad news. Very gently, I untied his leash, and he gave a little whimper as if to say, "Why are you doing that, Hank? I'm having fun."

"You're doing a great job, boy," I whispered to him. "But it's time for little dogs to take a rest."

I picked him up in my arms, but he wriggled out and went right back to his place in the line, wagging his tail. I scooped him up again.

"I'm really sorry, Cheerio. But remember, we're doing this for Mom."

He was still whimpering. This was really hard. Then I got a great idea. I carried him to the front of the line where Linus was waiting patiently.

"Hey, big guy," I said to him. "Do you mind if Cheerio rides with you?"

I put Cheerio down on Linus's back, just to test the idea. Linus didn't seem to mind. He didn't bark or try to shake Cheerio off. In fact, he turned his head around and gave him a friendly sniff. Cheerio seemed really happy up there on Linus's back, looking like a hood ornament on a classic car. He dug his paws into Linus's thick, white fur, and settled in just like he was on our couch at home.

"Is this okay with you?" I hollered to Harley.

"If it's okay with them, it's okay with me," he hollered back. "I just need to get moving."

I took Cheerio's leash and gently wrapped it around Linus's stomach to make sure Cheerio was nice and secure. Then I ran back to the sled as fast as I could.

Harley yelled mush, and the dogs tried to take off. But we were stuck in the snow. Maybe the sled had frozen to the ground.

"I'll get out and push," Harley said. "You hold the reins, kid."

Wow, that was exciting. Me, Hank Zipzer, Sled Driver of the Great North. I felt so proud that this guy I didn't even know was giving me such a big responsibility.

Harley pushed the sled with all his might. We still weren't moving, so my dad got out and pushed from the other side. The dogs were pulling as hard as they could. All of a sudden, with both men pushing and my dad's weight off the sled, we took off at full speed. There I was, holding the reins, and when I turned around, I saw my dad and Harley running after the sled.

What was I supposed to do? I didn't have much choice except to hang on.

"Hank!" Emily screamed. "Slow down!"

"If you have any idea how to do that, let me know NOW!" I shouted back.

We were careening down the off-ramp of the highway. I couldn't turn us back onto the road. The dogs were going where they wanted to go. When I looked up, I saw the Dairy Queen at the bottom of the off-ramp getting closer and closer. We were zooming downhill and right into the drive-through lane.

If there was ever a bad time for ice cream, trust me, this was it!

CHAPTER 22

I don't know what I did or didn't do, but I must have done something right because, all of a sudden, we came to an abrupt stop in front of the pickup window of the drive-through. Cheerio must have smelled the hamburger meat inside, because he started yipping as if he was ordering a double-double cheeseburger with a side of chili fries.

"Hank! Emily! Are you okay?" my dad hollered as he came running to the sled.

Harley followed right behind him.

"Look at that baby," he said.

I looked around to see what he was referring to. Was it Jean-Claude the poodle or Linus the husky?

It was neither. He was pointing to the sled.

"She's a fine ride," he said. "She can take an off-ramp at top speed and not even tip over."

He looked at me, and put his big hand on my shoulder and squeezed. It was no little squeeze—I thought I was going to have to say good-bye to my shoulder forever. I did all I could not to scream "ouch."

"You got some future in dogsled racing, kid," Harley said.

"Thanks anyway, Harley, but I don't think I'm going to do this again for a while."

I was pretty relieved when Harley took the reins and I could go sit in the backseat. My heart was pounding so hard that I thought it just might keep up that pace for the next three months.

I'd like to tell you that the rest of the trip was that exciting, but thank goodness, it wasn't. The biggest excitement was my dad checking his watch every two seconds and clearing his throat in that nervous way he does. I don't want it to get on your nerves the way it got on mine, so let me cut this short and just tell you that we arrived at Harley's mechanic in the Bronx exactly two hours, four minutes, and four hundred and thirty-three glances at the watch later.

CHAPTER 23

We said good-bye to Harley as he hurried into the auto parts store to pick up his fuel pump. He shook my hand so hard I thought it was going to go the same place my shoulder went. And once again, I didn't say "ouch." All I said was, "You're the man, Harley. Can I have my hand back now?"

We tried to unhitch Cheerio from the leash but he was so sad to leave his new friends that we had trouble getting him to let go of Linus's back. I think he wanted to become a permanent part of the team. I made a mental note to let him watch the Discovery Channel when the big sled race across Alaska was on.

My dad suggested that we go into the bakery that was right next to the auto parts store. It was called Stein's and, in gold lettering across the whole front window, it said: "World Famous

Butter Cake." I was so hungry that my mouth started to water just looking at the words. I was ready to eat the sign.

Inside, we ordered three cups of hot chocolate with marshmallows and three slices of their butter cake, which they served on paper plates. I don't know what was in that cake, but whatever it was, it sure got our brains working. We all started talking at once with our mouths full.

"Let's call a cab," my dad suggested.

"Good. We'll tell him to take us right to the hospital," I agreed.

"The cell phone is dead, remember?" Emily reminded us.

"So we can't even call your mother," Dad said.

"I hope we get there in time. Do you think she's waiting for us?" I asked.

"Statistically speaking, third babies arrive more quickly than one and two," Emily answered.

Dad and I both stared at her. I mean, it's not normal for a ten-year-old person to know a thing like that.

"What?" she said. "I researched it. You should try it sometime, Hank."

"Why? So I can turn out like you and grow pigtails and fall in love with an iguana? No thank you."

While we were arguing, my dad went to the counter and asked the woman if we could use their phone to call a taxi. He came back to our table with a sad look on his face. Even his pom-poms seemed droopy and depressed.

"She said not to bother because there are no taxis," he reported. "Several customers before us have tried to get one, but no luck. The storm has forced all the taxis back to the garage."

This news was not good. I could tell my dad was really losing it. He didn't even come up with another idea. He just starting pacing, and of course, clearing his throat.

"I got it," I said. "Let's call Mom on her cell."

"She's kind of busy right now, genius," Emily said. "As in she's having a baby."

"Okay, then let's call Papa Pete. Maybe one of his bowling pals can give us a ride."

My dad must have thought this was a good

idea, because he raced right over to the phone at the counter and dialed.

Papa Pete didn't answer.

"Okay," I said. "No need to panic. Let's call the Wongs. They have a car."

We did. They didn't answer.

"Okay," I said. "No problem. Let's call Frankie's mom on her cell."

We did. She didn't answer.

"Okay, let's call Frankie at home." I hoped he was there, because I was running out of people to call.

We dialed his number. And he answered!

My dad handed the phone to me. "Frankie," I said. "I'm so glad you're there. We're stuck in a bakery in the Bronx and we need a ride into the city."

"Dude, your mom's in the hospital. You got to get there right away."

"That's why I'm calling. Can your dad come pick us up?"

"He's at a conference on African masks," Frankie said. "I'm just here alone, except for Nick McKelty, which is basically like being alone."

"McKelty! You let that creep into your house? Does it smell? What's he doing there?"

"Science project. We're partners, remember?"

"Oh, right. Adolf stuck you with him. I remember now."

"Hold on a minute. The big lug is talking to me."

Frankie covered the phone and I could hear the muffled voice of Nick McKelty. You recognize it right away because it sounds thick and dull, like someone talking with a mouthful of doughnut holes, which he usually has oozing out between his teeth.

"Zip," Frankie said. "McKelty says he can help."

"Don't tell me," I said. "His father's got a friend who pilots a private jet that is able to land in the middle of a street in a snowstorm." That's the McKelty Factor, truth times a hundred. McKelty claims his dad knows everyone who can do anything at any time anywhere in the world. If that's the truth, then as Frankie says, my name is Bernice.

I heard Frankie turn to McKelty and say,

"Seriously, dude. This is an emergency. You have got to come through."

Before I knew it, McKelty's voice was on the phone.

"Listen, Zipperbutt," he said. "My dad is best friends with the guy who runs transportation for the entire city of New York. I'll call and ask him to send a vehicle for you. The guy owes my dad plenty."

Frankie must have grabbed the phone back because he said to me, "Call us back in five minutes. Let's give McKelty a chance to call his dad and prove himself."

Then the phone went dead.

"What happened?" my dad said.

"McKelty thinks he can help us. We'll know in five minutes."

Boy, it was a long five minutes we waited there in Stein's bakery. I was so nervous, I had another piece of butter cake and didn't even taste the butter.

At exactly five minutes, we called.

"It's a done deal," Frankie said. "Guido is the driver and he's on his way. He'll take you right to the hospital."

"Wow," I said. "This is great. More than great. This is fantasmagoric."

I hung up the phone and shook my head in amazement.

"What is fantasmagoric, Hank?" Emily asked. "Spill it!"

"You're not going to believe this, guys. Nick 'the bully' McKelty is sending a limousine for us."

I couldn't believe it myself. The guy who makes my life miserable actually came through. That was the good news. The bad news was that he was going to hold this over my head for the rest of my life, or even longer.

CHAPTER 24

We stood outside Stein's bakery to watch for the limousine. It wasn't hard, because very few cars were going by at all. In fact, there were fewer than few, as in zero.

"Do you think it will be a black stretch limo?" Emily asked. "Or a white one?"

"I hope it's not a white one," I answered, "because it will be hard to see it in the snow."

"This is awfully kind of your friend Nick McKelty," my dad said. "You'll have to be sure and write him a thank-you note."

The thought of writing a thank-you note in general makes me sick to my stomach. But add to that the fact that the note was going to Nick the Tick . . . well, my stomach started to do flip-flops right there in the Bronx. I felt my belly button smash against my belt buckle several times.

We waited in silence, watching eagerly for the limo. After a while, I saw a vehicle approaching. It was hard to make out exactly what it was because snow was falling again.

"Do you think that's him?" Emily asked.

I squinted into the distance, and now I could make out the shape of the vehicle. It was a garbage truck and it looked like a huge, blue, snow-eating beetle crawling its way toward us. When it pulled up alongside where we were standing, the driver rolled down his window and shouted out to us.

"Yous guys waitin' for me?"

"Oh no, sir," my dad said. "The only garbage we have is these empty hot chocolate cups."

"We're waiting for a limousine," I added, "to take us to the hospital."

"Yeah, that's where I'm going," the driver said. "Lenox Hill Hospital, right?"

"You're not Guido by any chance, are you?" I couldn't imagine that his answer would be yes.

"That's my name, don't wear it out," he said.

In my mind, I replayed the conversation that

I had with Nick the Tick. As I reviewed it, I realized that he hadn't actually said he was sending a limousine. What he said was that his father's friend was head of *transportation* for the city and he would send a *vehicle*. How typical of McKelty to make it sound like something it wasn't. I'll bet his dad's friend was the head of the garbage pickup and, naturally, the vehicle he sent for us was a dump truck!

Just another example of the McKelty Factor at work, folks.

I'm sure my dad saw the disappointment on my face. After what we had been through that day . . . the horse car, the acrobats' van, the dogsled . . . I was really looking forward to sitting on a soft seat with a heater and okay . . . maybe a moon roof and bottled water.

"We have to be grateful to have any ride at all," my father warned. "And remember, we're almost there."

Guido opened the door of the truck cab.

"Climb aboard," he said. "It's going be tight, but hey, we're all practically relatives, right? If you're close with McKelty, you're all right with me."

The reason it was going to be so tight in there was that two girls about four years old who looked exactly alike were sitting next to Guido, each one strapped into a car seat. They took up almost the whole front seat.

"These are my twins, Ratchlet and Colette," he explained. "The babysitter didn't show up so they're riding with me today. They love my truck, don't you, girls?"

"No!" Ratchlet said.

"It stinks," Colette pointed out.

And boy were they right. The cab was filled with the smell of years and years of people's garbage. I can't really describe it, but if you're ever in the neighborhood of a trash dumpster and want to give it a sniff . . . you might come close to the aroma that was curling my nose hairs.

"How about if the girl and the dog ride up here with us," Guido suggested. "You's guys can ride in back."

I looked toward the back of the truck. All I could see was plastic trash bags filled with who-knows-what, mixed in with piles of assorted tin cans and scraps of every kind of metal you could ever think of.

"Excuse me, Guido," I said, "but I don't see any seats back there."

"You don't need seats," Guido said. "Use the handles. Just hang on. The fresh air will do you good. We have to go slow in this weather, so don't worry, it's not dangerous."

Emily climbed into the front seat. Cheerio settled right into her lap and closed his eyes. Lucky dog. I sure wished I could take a nap in the front seat.

"Have a nice ride," Emily said. "Hope it's not too cold back there. Too bad you can't sit up here."

"That's okay. At least I won't have to sit next to you."

"Can I pull your pig tails?" Ratchlet said to Emily.

I saw her reach her little hand up to Emily's dangling hair.

"Me too!" echoed Colette. "I want a turn."

They were laughing like goons and, as I climbed down from the cab, I heard Emily screaming.

"Not so hard, girls. Those things are attached."

The twins laughed even louder, and I heard Guido say, "Hey, ladies. I taught you better than that. Act your age."

My dad and I went to the back of the truck and found two little metal platforms that were welded on to the sides. Above each one was a handle for the garbage collector to hold on to while he was standing on the platform, so he could jump on and off the truck to empty each trash can on the route.

"Hold on tight," my dad said, as he helped me climb up onto my platform.

"Maybe you should take your hat off," I suggested to him. "You don't want to get your pom-poms caught in the trash compactor."

And so we were off, bumping and thumping our way into New York City.

I wish I could tell you that the ride was really fun and interesting, but those aren't the first two words that spring to my mind. The first word that pops into my head to describe the ride is smelly. And the second one is stinky.

Just as a general rule, you don't want to be riding downwind of a garbage truck. As I hung onto the handle in the back, the combined smell of all the garbage wafted right up into my nose. Because I'm a nice guy, I'm going to spare you all the gory details, but let's just say that my nose got a major workout that afternoon. By the time we got to the hospital, about forty-five minutes later, my poor little snout was totally exhausted.

"There it is!" my dad shouted as we rounded the corner onto 77th Street. "Hank, have you ever seen such a beautiful hospital?"

It was just a plain average building with a blue sign out in front, but I could really and truly understand why my dad thought it was so beautiful. Inside, my mom was waiting for us, about to give birth to a brand-new Zipzer.

Then suddenly it hit me. What if she already had?

CHAPTER 25

The very second Guido stopped the truck, my dad and I were on the street, running to the door of the hospital. Suddenly, I stopped dead in my tracks. We had forgotten something.

Someone, that is.

Emily, to be exact. And Cheerio.

We both realized it at exactly the same moment. As we ran back to Guido's truck, Emily was climbing down from the front seat, clutching onto a still sleepy Cheerio, with Guido holding her hand for support. The twins were a giggling mess, and shouting their little heads off.

"Good-bye, pig tails!" Ratchlet screamed.

"Toodle-oo, piggy hair!" giggled Colette.

Then they collapsed into laughter. Boy, four-year-olds sure are easily amused. Were they ever annoying. It made me think that the good thing about my new brother was that first off, he was a boy, and second off, there was only one of him.

We all shook Guido's hand and thanked him.

"It was so kind of you to come for us," my dad said.

"No problem," he answered. "Happy to do a favor for McKelty. We go way back, him and me."

"Do you know his son Nick?" I asked him. I just couldn't resist.

"Yeah," Guido said. "He's kind of a bum. Not really nice to my girls. Keeps taking their dessert. Maybe he'll shape up some day and be more like you. You gotta hope for that."

I knew there was something I really liked about this Guido: The man had good taste in people!

Guido waved good-bye and the three of us took off running for the hospital door. A receptionist was sitting at the front desk, and she told us we could find my mom on the third floor. We didn't even want to wait for the elevator.

"Where are the stairs?" my dad asked her.

"They're right next to the elevators," she said, "but I hope you're not planning to take that dog upstairs. We only allow animals that are service dogs or therapy dogs in the hospital."

"Cheerio is a therapy dog," I said. "He makes my mom feel really good."

We didn't wait for her answer, just bolted up the stairs like our feet had wings. On the third floor, a nice janitor directed us to the Maternity Waiting Room, which was behind a glass door at the end of the lime green hall.

We burst into the room, gasping for air like we were the ones having a baby. The room was empty except for one man sitting on a sofa reading the newspaper. We couldn't see his face because he was holding the newspaper up in front of it.

"Excuse me, sir," I said to him. "Do you know where the babies are born?"

When he lowered the newspaper, I realized the man was Papa Pete, my grandpa and the best person any of us could have seen at that moment.

"I'm so glad you're here," he said, giving Emily and me his usual bear hug.

"Am I too late?" my dad asked.

"She's in there," he said, pointing to a set of glass double doors. "You better hurry!"

After my dad went racing through the double doors, Emily, Papa Pete, and I sat there in the waiting room, waiting. I'm not so good at waiting, or sitting, but I am a good walker, so I got up and paced around the room making a batman design on the carpet with the soles of my sneakers.

"Hank," Papa Pete said. "Relax. Sit down. I brought you a snack. Your favorite. A crunchy dill."

"Thanks, Papa Pete, but this isn't exactly a pickle moment. I'm kind of worried about Mom. Will she be okay?"

"She was okay when she had you," Papa Pete said. "And she was okay when she had your sister. I think she's pretty good at having babies by now."

Frankie's mom arrived from a coffee run she had made for Papa Pete. She was very relieved that my dad was in there with my mom.

"I'll leave you all to be a family now," she said.

We asked her if she would take Cheerio home. Poor guy. He was totally passed out under a chair, snoring louder than even Papa Pete does. He needed to be home in his doggy bed.

Mrs. Townsend hugged us, wished us luck, and left, carrying Cheerio in her backpack. We settled in to wait some more. Emily just sat there doing a crossword puzzle. Papa Pete had brought her a book of crossword puzzles and a new, pink mechanical pencil because she doesn't like pickles much. That shows how much her tongue knows.

I couldn't believe she could even try to come up with a seven-letter word for penguin toes at a time like this. Holy macaroni, she was turning into my dad right in front of my eyes. *Someone toss a bucket of water on her, quickly, and stop the transformation!* I saw that happen once in a horror movie where a guy was turning into a giant blood-sucking mosquito. The water dissolved him just in time.

I went back to tracing Batman in the carpet, and had just finished his cape when my dad came bursting through the double doors. I froze in my tracks. Batman was going to have to wait for his tights.

Sorry, Batman. Hope you don't catch a cold.

Papa Pete stood up, and even Emily dropped her new, pink mechanical pencil. You know something big is about to happen when that girl lets go of a mechanical pencil.

"First let me say," Dad boomed, not realizing his voice was so loud. "Mom is fine and so is your brother. And I am so glad we got here in time because that little guy was not waiting one more second."

"Hooray!" I screamed, my voice even louder than my dad's. "And, guess what? I've come up with the perfect name."

"Hank . . ." my dad interrupted, but I wasn't waiting for him. When you have an idea as sensational as I had, it's got to come out right away.

"We should name him after each person who helped us get here in time," I said. "So, let me announce the name of my little brother. It's Trigger Chin Harley Guido Zipzer. Is that the best name or what?"

"That is the stupidest, dumbest name I

have ever heard," Emily said. "For sure, we should name him Isaac after the world's greatest scientist, Sir Isaac Newton."

"That dude with the apples dropping on his head?" I said. "No way, Jose."

"Well, we're not naming him Trigger, I can tell you that," Emily shot back.

"Hank! Emily! Both of you!" my dad said. "Can I please get a word in here?"

"Let your dad finish his sentence," Papa Pete said. "This is very exciting. I'd like to know what he has to say."

"Sure, Dad, but make it fast because I want to go meet Trigger."

"I'm afraid you're going to have to save the name Trigger for your next pet spider," my dad said. "It's an excellent spider name."

"I don't know, Dad. It's really hard to picture putting a saddle on a spider. But I guess you could do it if you got a really little saddle. I mean, we're talking itty-bitty."

"Hank, stop and listen," my dad said.

"I'm back," I said. "I'm right with you, Dad."

"Good, because this is important. Your

mother and I have decided to call your brother Harry, after my father."

I was back, but was I ever sorry.

"You're kidding, Dad." The words just fell out of my mouth. "You have the chance to give this kid the name of the century, and you stick him with Harry?"

"Harry Irving Zipzer is a fine name."

"Dad, if you don't mind, I'm going to pretend I didn't hear that."

"Well, hear it, because that's his name."

"Harry is a short man who probably wears a bow tie."

"Harry is also a prince in England. A name is what you bring to it, Hank. And this Harry is our Harry who will bring the Zipzer attitude to whatever name we give him."

And then it hit me, all at once, and clearer than ever before. Harry Irving Zipzer was coming home with me, into my room, to mess up my things, to leave his poopy diapers in my wastebasket.

"Dad," I said, before I could stop my mouth. "Actually, now that I think about it, I don't think I want a brother. Is it too late to send him back where he came from?"

"Of course it is, moron," Emily said.

"Well, then," I went on, "maybe we can exchange him for an alien. That would be interesting. And they don't wear much. I could get my drawers back."

"Hank," Papa Pete said, putting his big hand on my shoulder. "Before you know it, you are going to having such a good time with Harry. He's going to look up to you for everything. Who's going to teach him how to zip up the zipper on his jacket?"

"I'm not very good at that myself," I said. "I keep getting my shirt caught in the stupid thing."

"Who wants to go say hi to your new brother?" my dad asked, finally untying the mask that was hanging around his neck. By the way, did I mention that he was still wearing his pom-pom hat? Well, he was.

"I do!" Emily said. "Katherine and I even made him a 'welcome to the world' card."

"One thing I know for sure," I said. "This baby is not interested in communicating with reptiles."

"Why don't we go ask him?" my dad said. "Come on, children."

Emily skipped after my dad as he pushed open the double doors that led down the hall to the hospital rooms. I hung back in the waiting room and just looked at Papa Pete. To be honest, I wasn't all that enthusiastic about meeting this kid.

"You have to trust me, Hank," Papa Pete said. "Having a little brother is going to be the greatest thing in the world."

I trusted Papa Pete's taste in pickles, that's for sure. But when it came to his advice about little brothers, I was having a really hard time digesting his idea.

ZIPZER!

CHAPTER 26

Papa Pete and I followed my dad and Emily down the hall to my mom's room, which, in case you're ever at Lenox Hill Hospital, was 5011. I was pretty nervous about going in and I stopped at the entrance. My feet felt like I had a cement block on each of my shoes. But Papa Pete gave me a little push in the small of my back, and before you could say Harry Irving Zipzer, I was in.

"Hank, honey," my mom said. "Come give me a hug. I really need one from my big guy."

My mom actually looked great. A little tired, but she seemed really happy. I gave her a hug, and then another one. Wow, she was in a hugging frenzy. The only bad thing was that she was hugging Emily, too, and on the third hug, our hair touched. That put an end to my hugging.

I worked my way out from under her arm

and looked around the bed. Then I looked around the room.

"So where is he?" I asked.

"They just took him to the nursery to give me a little break," my mom said.

Wow. This guy had only been on the planet for five minutes and already she needed a break. Imagine what it's going to be like having him live in my room?

I hope this doesn't make me seem selfish, but suddenly, out of nowhere, came a hunger pang in my stomach so bad, I thought I was going to faint. I needed a candy bar, and I needed it fast.

"Hey, Mom, how about if I come back in a few minutes when the baby returns?" I said. "I feel like checking out the hall."

"Sure, honey," my mom said. "Just don't make any noise, because the babies are sleeping and new moms need their rest, too."

As I flew out of there, I reached into my jeans pocket. Oh, please let there be enough money for a candy bar. I pulled out a handful of change and tried to count it. It was either eighty-six cents or sixty-eight cents. I couldn't figure it out for the life of me. My only choice was to find a candy machine, pump all the coins in, and see what came out.

"Excuse me," I said to a passing nurse. "Can you tell me where I might find a candy machine?"

"Sure, dear," she said. "Just go past the nursery and turn left."

Oh great. Not only could I not figure out how much money I had, I couldn't figure out the direction I needed to go in either. A double whammy, right there in the hospital hallway.

As I was heading down the hall, trying to figure out which way was right and which way was left, my eye caught the name Zipzer in a reflection from the hall window. I walked up to the window, and looked in. The window was a little high, and I had to stand on my tiptoes to see what was going on inside.

Wow, was I surprised. There were about ten babies, all wrapped up in pink or blue blankets, like Cabbage Patch dolls. They were in these plastic bins that looked like something Mr. Kim puts fruit in at his corner market. Each one had a sign with his or her name on it and that day's date. The third blue blanket from the end said: ZIPZER.

I stood on the very tips of my toes to look over the Zipzer sign, and here's what I saw: the pinkest, little face with the tiniest, little eyebrows you've ever seen. His eyes were closed, and he seemed to be pretty mellow.

Wow, that was Harry. I didn't want to make him feel bad, so let's just keep this between you and me. Harry could really have used some hair. He looked like a ping-pong ball with peach fuzz.

Suddenly, his eyes opened and he seemed to be checking out the room.

Wait a minute, he's not looking at the room. He's looking over my way. I'm pretty sure he's looking at me.

I started to wave.

Hey, Harry. Over here. It's Hank. We both have a first name that starts with an H.

Then his little mouth opened and his nose scrunched up like a bunny rabbit's.

What's that about, Harry? You don't want to make that face in front of too many people. I mean, you're cute and all, but don't push it.

Then his face turned beat red and his mouth opened even wider.

Uh-oh. He's crying. What's wrong, little buddy?

"Excuse me," I called out into the hall. "My brother is crying. Can somebody see what the problem is? Maybe he needs to burp."

No one answered, which made all kinds of sense because I was alone in the hallway.

Oh look. He's turning his head to check out his neighbor. His nametag said: BINH RILEY. There's a kid in my class named Binh. His parents are from Vietnam. Maybe this kid has relatives there, too.

Oh wow. Binh is looking at Harry.

I stood in the hall, wondering if babies can communicate with each other. What would they say?

Binh: *Yo, Harry. Could you pipe down? I'm trying to nap here.*

Harry: *Sorry, dude. I have an itch on my nose like you can't believe. Could you lean over and scratch it.*

Binh: *I would love to, but they have my arms tucked so tight in this blanket, I feel like the mummy from* The Curse of the Pyramids.

Harry: *Are you hungry, or is it just me? I hear all you get is milk in this place. I could go for a cheeseburger.*

Binh: *Yeah, my stomach is starting to growl. So where are you from, anyway?*

Harry: *I'm not sure. But I heard them say I have a sister and a brother.*

Binh: *A brother? That's cool. I've only got a sister and a kitten.*

Harry: *Yeah, I can't wait to meet my brother. I hear he's so cool.*

Suddenly, I knocked on the nursery window.

"Hey, Harry, here I am," I said out loud. This time I was really glad the hallway was empty. "You really want to meet me? You really think I'm cool? That's great because I got a lot of fun things planned for us."

I felt a hand gently touch my shoulder. It was Papa Pete.

"Who are you talking to, Hank?"

"Harry," I said to him. "He's a pretty outgoing little guy. He's already made a new friend."

Papa Pete raised his eyebrows and smiled.

"So you and Harry are getting along okay?"

"Yeah. Don't tell anyone, but I think I kind of like him."

"So you're getting used to the idea of sharing your room with him?"

"As a matter of fact, I can't wait for him to come home. And I've decided that someday, I might even let him wear my Mets sweatshirt."

Before Papa Pete could answer, a nurse came in and walked right up to Harry's little, plastic bed. She unlocked the wheels and mouthed to us that she was taking him back to my mom.

I could have sworn I saw Harry turn to Binh and say, "See you in preschool, buddy."

As the nurse wheeled Harry down the hall, I skipped along right behind her, happily following my new little brother to my mom's room where the whole family was waiting to meet him.

About the Authors

HENRY WINKLER is an actor, producer, director, coauthor, public speaker, husband, father, brother, uncle, and godfather. He lives in Los Angeles with his wife, Stacey. They have three children named Jed, Zoe, and Max, and three dogs named Monty, Charlotte, and Linus. He is so proud of the Hank Zipzer series that he could scream—which he does sometimes, in his backyard!

If you gave him two words to describe how he feels about the Hank Zipzer series, he would say: "I am thrilled that Lin Oliver is my partner and we write all these books together." Yes, you're right, that was sixteen words. But, hey! He's got learning challenges.

LIN OLIVER is a writer and producer of movies, books, and television series for children and families. She has created over one hundred episodes of television, four movies, and over twelve books. She lives in Los Angeles with her husband, Alan. They have three sons named Theo, Ollie, and Cole, and a very adorable but badly behaved puppy named Dexter.

If you gave her two words to describe this book, she would say "funny and compassionate." If you asked her what "compassionate" meant, she would say "full of kindness." She would not make you look it up in the dictionary.